Recognition

Recognition

Janet Killeen

authorHOUSE®

AuthorHouse™ UK Ltd.
1663 Liberty Drive
Bloomington, IN 47403 USA
www.authorhouse.co.uk
Phone: 0800.197.4150

This is a work of fiction. All of the characters, names, incidents, organizations, and dialogue in this novel are either the products of the author's imagination or are used fictitiously.

Published by AuthorHouse   05/07/2013

ISBN: 978-1-4817-9411-4 (sc)
ISBN: 978-1-4817-9413-8 (hc)
ISBN: 978-1-4817-9412-1 (e)

Library of Congress Control Number: 2013908326

Any people depicted in stock imagery provided by Thinkstock are models, and such images are being used for illustrative purposes only.
Certain stock imagery © Thinkstock.

This book is printed on acid-free paper.

Contents

For my Friends, with love and gratitude

Recognition

They met once.
Early on a shining day
As the sun rose pearl and silver,
Before the heat and dust
Pressed down on travellers, and slowed the pace.

Where roads joined and flowed together,
Glimpsed across
      The backs of laden animals
And sweating, purposed faces of the crowd,
Their faces mirrored recognition.
A quiet knowledge of a different destination
And a travelled road:
Not measured
In these dusty footprints
Or the weary paces of driven animals,
But in the steps of years,
The eroding rock,
The scouring watercourse:
The huge journeys of time.

Each seeing fully in that moment
      Of indrawn breath and wonder
The other's unseen secret:
The mother of the prophet,
The great-grandmother of kings.

© Janet Killeen 2013

Dust

The spoken words were for her. I heard them, quiet though they were, in the immense stillness of the noon heat. But the words lettered in the dust and brushed away, those words were for me. In all that turmoil, I read them and knew their meaning. Now, I remember down the long years' perspective the sharp details of that day.

The heat strikes down in vertical columns towards midday, bringing work to a halt. Dogs gasp in shadowed corners, donkeys struggle with their loads to reach the shade of trees. The streets and squares empty themselves of all save slaves and beggars. Imagine the palpable blows of the sun, like a great hammer driving piles into the earth, and the silence as the everyday traffic of the town recedes and the heat fills the emptiness with itself. Then hear, distant at first, then lurching and dragging round corners, the hoarse cry of a crowd: triumph and contempt mingled in some way that is, even now as I hear it in my memory, less than human. Frightening. Feral.

There in the outer court, picked out by the white glare of the light with blue-black shadows crouching beneath them, a crowd of men. Robes, phylacteries, tassels swirling with the passionate energy that had brought them together, and in the midst of them, dragged and now thrown onto the paving stones, a young woman. Dishevelled, her robe ripped at the breast, panting, gulping with pain and terror. My wife. They force her to stumble to her feet and she stands, swaying, plucking helplessly at her clothes, before a man sitting in the colonnade. The crowd of men swells, shouting, jeering, gesticulating, then falling silent to wait for his response. And I, walking home from the Temple site, with my stone mason's hammer over my shoulder, meeting them at that angle of the courtyard.

I could smell their potency, a mixture of hate and lust, directed at her and through her to the man who stepped from the bench in the shade of the pillars and bent down to squat on his heels in the dust near to her. *Caught in the very act!* The rankness of their sweat and haste caused their garments to stick to their bodies as they stood, leaning forwards, silent now. Their knuckles fused to the rocks they carried. I could not see her face, could not push through the barrier of their purpose. I could only see the man, bent before her, drawing shapes with his finger, writing in the dust. Where was her lover, that young merchant's son? I had known of him, but pretended wearily not to know. He was nowhere near: running, no doubt, from the bed as the crowd approached, taking refuge in his father's money to flee the town.

Was it inevitable, this moment of exposure and the months of unfaithfulness that led to it? Even now, years later, I wonder if it could have been different. Who and what we are is hidden deep within the core of us, as it is when you split the rock and find crystal beauty or hidden flaw or strength to sustain the weight of the building. Only that testing, splitting pressure can show us ourselves. I was approaching thirty, a master mason, working on the Jerusalem Temple site. My work was a joy to me, as I believe it is to all craftsmen, and I look back now on the miracle of that gleaming Temple rising into the sky, a glory of light and air created from marble so brilliant that it seemed to magnify the very light of the sun. After my foot was crushed under a block of stone I could no longer climb the upper scaffolding walkways but I worked on the carvings of pomegranate and vine and loved what I did. The sharp precision of the chisel exploring the rock, the release of curve and beauty as the flower and leaf and fruit take shape. You would call me quiet, I think, perhaps retiring, absorbed in what my hands were making.

She was young, too young at fifteen years to be betrothed to a man nearly twice her age. Her father, I remember, eager to marry her off, the young daughter left on his hands when his wife died. There was little love in that home, and she was thrust out into marriage. I could provide for a wife with a good home, a maid servant for her, respect in the village. And I loved her. She was beautiful beyond my describing; but a wild creature trapped, I realised when I married her. Obedient, frightened, often hiding from me at first: then her fear became anger, scorn for me in my clumsy attempts to reach her. I had no skill to win or please her. I did not, could not know even how to speak with her. After the accident, she did not hide her contempt: *I had no choice in marrying you,* she said, *and now you are lame.* A door closed between us. Perhaps it would have helped if there had been a child in those early years, but I would not wish a child to have been conceived in contempt or reluctance. So it was. I, absorbed in my work, she alone, angry, afraid, desperate. It is no wonder that she was drawn to a young man who gave her excitement, the pleasure of her youth and dreams again. As I have said, I knew, but chose not to know. I saw the looks, heard the whispers, but hoped somehow I might find her again when this had run its course. Never, never would I have brought her to a place of shame. That moment in the Temple court tore across both our lives.

I had been working since dawn: you work in the early hours while the light is pearl and gentle. The blinding white of the marble would burn the eye in the full glare of the day. So I was returning to the village, crossing the court of the Gentiles at a tangent to leave by the gate to the Kidron Valley. I remember noticing very distinctly in the silence a scuttering lizard on the wall and the arcing swallows high overhead. Then the murmur, eager, almost greedy, which swelled again to demand an answer. I saw the man, bent before her, so that in her shame and terror he was lower than her, creating a small circle of safety around her as he continued to draw their eyes away from her exposed and trembling body to the words he inscribed and then smoothed away in the dust between them. The silence again: palpable, quivering in the heat. He rose to his feet to look round at the circle of men, holding their gaze, one by one. *If you're sure you've never done wrong,* he said, almost carelessly, *you could throw the first stone.*

Then he bent down again, and continued his writing. A strange unease, almost embarrassment, passed like a spasm among the crowd, and then they moved away, each remembering some other purpose. When they had gone, he stood up again, drawing her eyes and lifting her head with his gaze—eye to eye, as no other man would look at a woman unless related to her. *So where are they, then,* he asked her gently, *those who would have condemned you?*

I saw her draw together all the frail and shattered pieces of her bid for freedom, wings smashed against the bars of her life—a loveless childhood and marriage, the humiliation of her exposure, her powerlessness as a woman. All of that degradation was held, absorbed, cancelled in the exchange of look for look that passed between them. *They are not here, Sir,* she answered. I do not know whether she knew that I was present or not. *Then you too, you are free to go. And you can walk free of past shame.*

Suddenly released, I moved forward from my rigid place in the shadows, my outer cloak ready in my hand to cover her from the stares of strangers as we returned home. She turned to see me, and, as though for the first time, we saw each other clearly, look for look, as I walked to her. And I glimpsed again the words in the dust, before the man bent and brushed them away. *Go, love . . . again.* Words from the prophet Hosea.

I have often wondered how it was that the finger of God wrote upon the stone tablets of Moses. Were the words incised with fire, chiselled out of living rock? Or what of the fingers that wrote upon the wall of Belshazzar? I saw the finger of God here, lean, brown, a workman's hand much like my own, and it spelled out healing not judgement.

And so we left Jerusalem and its neighbourhood. There is always work for a mason, even with a crippled foot, and so we travelled first to Caesarea Philippi where I found work on the summer palace. Soon, we moved to Corinth, seeking a new beginning and a new community, and gradually love, trust, kindness grew between us. Shame fled away, and our children were born. And our first born, our daughter, your mother, we called Keziah, after Job's daughter, that she would always have an equal inheritance with her brothers.

It is now many years since my dear wife died. All our years of healing and happiness have long outweighed those early griefs, but I want you to understand and remember our story. Make sure that it is told, so that others understand how she was treated on that day, and how he raised her up to dignity and hope. It is forty years ago, and now Jerusalem itself has fallen into ruin. Those magnificent walls besieged, and the stone blocks, so crisply carved and joined that you could not pass a feather between them, all crashed into rubble, split, wrecked. A desolation. But what was written in the dust remains.

Twelve Years

I thought for a few moments that she was up to her usual tricks. Tired, stubborn and insistent on returning to a quiet corner of the field and an unburdened evening. I patted her neck, affectionate and exasperated, and called to Joel who walked quietly behind me. But as I dropped down from the saddle and she moved awkwardly away from me I saw she was lame and hobbling and needed to be led back home. We were four miles from the town now and I was uncertain what to do. This gentle wander through familiar countryside faltered: my wish had been to remember, to savour the aloneness, to ready myself for the wedding next month. All its excitement and mystery lay before me: a man well-chosen whom I was sure I could grow to love, a wedding feast that would stir the whole community to celebration. I knew that it marked the end of choices—the choice to be alone, to follow my own impulses. The end, too, of the immediate closeness of an only daughter and her parents. I saw the cost of that sometimes in the ways they looked at me and at each other when they thought I was preoccupied. For the past five years there had been that anguished, grateful murmur, 'We so nearly lost you'.

'Please. Sit here in the shade while you wait. Here against the wall. It is cool here under the fig tree even on the hottest day.'

A strong welcoming voice, and a woman stepped from a trellised doorway into the lane. Brown crinkled face and hands, black clothing, liquid eyes that surprised me with their recognition. I had never seen her before, or if I had I had never noticed, but now there was a steady intensity which held me: it was safe and kind and I knew what was best to do. I sent Joel home with my poor lamed donkey and asked him to return with another, and one for himself, and to tell my parents where I was. 'At Hannah's house in the village', she said to him. 'She can wait with me until you return.'

I looked around the little courtyard. Lavender and yellow-flowered sage grew in pots in the corners and the afternoon sun brought their scent to me. In the corner, an old fig tree spread its plump-fingered leaves over the yard and doves floated above and settled back to their cote. I had not realised until I sat down how restless I had become; a stranger to myself. I leaned against the stone wall, glad of its sturdy roughness and of the deep shade that hid me.

'I will bring you something to drink,' she said. 'I have ewe's milk from my own flock, or water from the spring. And there are raisins and honey cakes.'

'Thank you,' I said, slowly. 'The ewe's milk would be lovely. It reminds me of childhood. But please sit beside me and eat with me.'

'You do not know me,' she stated, drawing her skirts comfortably around her as she sat down and placed two cups and a plate of cakes and fruit on the wall beside us.

'No,' I answered. What else could I say? Here was a stranger: gentle, welcoming, utterly familiar.

She drew her finger through the dust in front of us—a winding track, perhaps, and then another alongside which crossed the first. The quietness settled.

'I remember your birth,' she said. 'News from the town travels quickly and your father is well-known and respected. They had waited many years, your parents, and their joy was infectious. For me, it was a different kind of beginning. Or ending.'

I sat still with my hands cupped in my lap. She stirred and spoke again. 'I had a string of miscarried babies. So many hopes and losses. I was married at fifteen. Ten years. And then, the bleeding would not stop.' She flinched as if remembering, then looked at me. 'It was around the time of your birth, and I remember so well the news on everyone's tongue and my own secret sense of cruel disappointment. I thought it was another miscarriage, but it went on and on. My husband was a good man. He sent for doctors, took me to the town, spent all that we had on cures and medicines. All the money from the flock, everything that could be spared. You will understand how it was. I became untouchable. Friendships died, my husband became a stranger to me. I could not go to the synagogue or join the festivals. I hid myself, consumed with the dragging pain, the uncleanness, the daily struggle to manage. Even the smell of myself, the shame. When my husband died, I paid a herdsman to tend the few goats left and kept myself within this courtyard. Sometimes some kind soul would tell me of a new doctor or a new remedy and I would sell a goat and pay for treatments that I knew were worthless.' She unexpectedly smiled. 'The more revolting the medicine, the more effective it promised to be.'

The sun had moved the shadows across the yard. We sat comfortably together. Her voice spoke truth but lacked all bitterness in its remembering.

'This little space became a place of hope to me. I planted herbs and flowers, kept doves, watched the stars after nightfall. My husband had planted a vine which gave grapes and the old fig tree never ceased to bear fruit. You have to look for God elsewhere if they won't let you in. I found him in the daily pleasure of flowers breaking from bud, the colour of dawn skies, the gentleness of those doves' calls. I waited for twelve years.'

I also remembered my twelfth year, but through a haze of sickness and fever, and the sudden awakening to a clear calm voice, my father and mother bending over me, crying, and four strangers in the room. The voice was like light, piercing through the dark and stuffy room and its hangings that smothered me with heat. The grip of the hand pulled me up from the darkness: 'Little girl, it's time to wake up!' After the nightmare of sickness, the ordinariness of the next words: 'She needs something to eat'. Unforgettable. Life-giving.

'He was on his way to your father's house.' Her brown finger traced the path in the dust again and I saw how we were coming together. 'Your father had begged him to come and heal you. Everyone had heard of him and there was a great crowd around him. Curious, desperate, impatient people. Many were strangers, and I knew that I could hide among them if I covered my face and swathed myself in the clothes of widowhood. One more widow among so many. If they had known, of course, who was touching them in the crowd and making them unclean, they would have thrown me off the road, stoned me perhaps. I think I had become so quietly desperate, maybe a little unhinged, that the risk was meaningless to me.'

I moved so that my right hand took her left and held it to my cheek and she smiled. 'I did a thing so terrible and so wonderful that I cannot now imagine how I did it. I pressed through the crowd—I shoved and heaved to get my way! I had hardly been touched in twelve years and now I forced my way through the crowd until I saw him—not his face, I didn't dare—his back. I said to myself, if I can touch even the edge of his clothes I can be healed. I know this man carries the healing power of God and he's nothing to do with the rules and regulations of the temple and the priests. As I touched his clothes, I knew. It was as if the coolness of deep well water washed me. Clean, wholesome, alive. I felt,' she laughed with the memory, 'Young again'.

We laughed together, watching the doves rise up startled and settle murmuring again. 'I wanted to run, to laugh and sing and dance again, the things you do when you are young and carefree. I started to push my way out of the crowd, but his voice stopped me. "Who touched me? I know that I've given healing power to someone. Who is it?"

Now, I was terrified! I fell down in the dust, but I had to confess it was me and look him in the face and tell him all that I had been through and how I had dared to touch him. And he looked round, and the crowd was muttering and some of them were saying it was a disgrace and twitching their clothes in case I had touched them. He took hold of my hand and said a strange thing: "My Daughter." He looked at me as if all my history was known to him and I was being praised in front of the whole crowd: "It's your faith that has made you well. Now you can be at peace." The muttering died down and the crowd made room for me to pass. And as I did so, messengers from your father's house came running up, saying you were dead, and not to bother the Teacher any more. Your poor father. He had waited while Jesus dealt with me and he must have been desperate. Now it looked as if my healing was at your expense. It was too late. But I heard the Teacher's voice again, "Don't be afraid. Have faith. She will be well." And you were. Your story was in everyone's mouths by the morning.'

I looked at her, and felt the stability of her peace, the wonder of a pathway of so much pain turned to wholesomeness and the miracle of this encounter. Or I saw it as streams that flow fresh down the mountainside after the winter snows have melted and run to join one another.

'So, I have waited for this meeting,' she said. 'I knew that one day we would stop for a little time and speak. You, who so nearly died on the day that my life was given back to me. As if I were not childless somehow, but part of your rebirth.' She paused. 'News came to us two years later from Jerusalem of a terrible death, but also of a great mystery. There were many who said that he appeared alive on the third day. I believe that. The power that healed and the kindness that spoke to me on that day could not be kept in a tomb.

I sometimes imagine that he will walk down this lane for me one day, at my life's end and speak to me again. "Daughter".'

She laughed again. 'No-one else has called me that in more than thirty years.'

I heard the sound of hooves approaching down the lane.

'I will fetch your man some water,' she said. 'Before you go.'

'Thank you,' I answered. 'For all you have given me today. Will you come and bless me at my wedding?'

'I will come,' she said.

Out of the Storm

When I was around nine years old and the beatings became very bad I discovered that I could fly out of my body and leave it behind. I watched it, as a bird in a tree far above might watch a distant creature on the ground. Its movements were not my movements, nor its sobs my sobs, and the pain went away into a small place inside my head which I could not feel anymore. I stayed safe in the tree of my mind until it was over and I could return in the darkness and teach myself that it could be borne.

I have little memory of earlier days of childhood. A father dead and his widow and child sold for his debts. A man who took the widow and child away, but despised the child, silencing the widow, I now see, by his lies. I was not taken into the house of his friend to learn the skills of a household servant but thrown out. A beggar on the streets of the town, desperate for scraps and coins. Knowing no-one, I learned then how to plead with my eyes, to elbow through crowds to be the first to hold the horse's head for a penny or to extend the hollowed hand to beg from a woman who looked pityingly at me. In the corners of outbuildings or the ancient roots of trees I found shelter until the day a travelling seller of trinkets picked me up, a homeless boy to carry his bundle. He promised a full belly and clothes for my back and I went with him.

Hunger and knocks were familiar to me, but this man was different. At times, kind, smiling, generous, but then turning in an instant to rage, seizing me in one rigid hand and dealing blows to my head and chest with the other as I squirmed away. Later, he took

14

a stick and the beatings became a regular part of the wandering life that we led: it made no difference whether nothing had been sold or whether there had been enough for him to buy the rough acid wine of the region. He lost control over himself and turned in some ugly dull rage to hit me, his face coarse and mottled and spit flying from his mouth as he shouted and lashed out. Always, part of me watching, even when the pain broke through and I squirmed free and crouched sobbing on the ground at a distance. There was nowhere I could go, and even if I turned again to begging, this region east of the Lake was strange to me, a dialect I could barely understand, sparse and poor villages with unkind and unwelcoming eyes. So I discovered my secret. That when the pain became too bad to be borne, I could become a bird and leave my body behind. And watch him, and watch myself, and wait. Later the bruises and the blood could be taken to the stream and bathed. Perhaps there would be several days when I could heal. There might be food to cram into an empty belly, and the man might turn kind with a flash of the old laugh and a share of the takings. So I lived, trapped between his sudden angry violence and his strange impulses of generosity, until I was old enough to run away.

He had renewed his stock in the town and turned south. I was twelve or maybe thirteen, thin but strong, defiant, suspicious, waiting now for the moment when I could see the possibility of escape from him and the chance to find a living for myself. We came at the end of one afternoon to a village, one of so many villages. The dogs, half wild, set up their barking as we approached. Thin goats were tethered under trees, guarded by urchins much like myself. Women, black-clad, hefted the heavy pitchers at the well and turned to their meagre houses. And the streets, dust and dung, past the dark doorways. Children, huge-eyed, gathered as he set up his display of glitter on a wall near the village centre, and the women clustered. One or two of the men shouldered in and one, with smile at a pretty girl across the street, bent to choose a gift for her. I watched the strange normality of it all, the children eager and impressed with the magic of a stranger, the women chattering and laughing, the young man smiling at the girl as if all the world hung on this moment of giving. I felt myself edging away, as if my body knew what my mind could not admit, that these bonds of kindness, poor and ordinary as they were, could never be mine. And I slid into the shadows and fled.

All day and as twilight deepened into blackness I stumbled over the high herdsmen's paths to put many ridges of hills between me and his pursuit, sleeping at last in the early hours of dawn. I woke to cling to the skirts of a woman who was sitting quietly under the trees waiting for me as her goats nibbled among the grasses. A very old and toothless woman with sharp eyes buried in a maze of wrinkles as she smiled. She took my hand and led me into her small house and gave me goat's milk, warm from the udder, and a bannock of coarse bread. She asked no questions but pushed me towards a pile of skins and I slept, I think, all that day and night and woke only as the grey light of early morning stirred the birds and I heard her busyness kindling a fire and grinding flour. I awoke for the first time in all my memory without fear.

She brought water to wash me and soak off the rags of my clothes, laughing gently as I tried to cover myself and muttering to herself as she touched the bruises and wheals on my back and the cuts and grazes of my feet. She rubbed them with some mixture of herb and oil and found me clothes. It was for her as though her long-dead son had come again.

'What is your name?' she asked in the patois of the region.

I knew enough to say to her, 'I do not know. He called me "boy".'

'The Widow has her son again,' the village said, some with kindness. I stayed to tend her flock and mend the house walls and roof. I turned the earth in her small patch and planted and watered so that we could eat together, poor enough food but more than I could ever remember, and seasoned always with the grace of her loving. For many months I woke in the night to the startle and shudder of my cries and she would hush me as though I were a little child again. She called me 'son' and sometimes the name of her dead boy, and I loved her. I found a place of belonging in her home and even some villagers nodded a greeting, and I began to mend. For five years I followed the slow, safe rhythms of the soil and the flock until one dawn I found her stiff and already cold when I rose. I buried her, not among the cave tombs, but at the edge of the field where she had found me, covering her carefully with stones, and walked up into the hills to mourn. Late, late that evening I turned back to the village, aware somewhere at the edge of my mind that the bird of watching had returned, and was waiting. I crept into the house, sleeping exhausted until I was roused by voices calling me in the early morning.

'You have no claim to this house or land,' a man said, harshly, a man I had seen demanding rent from the Widow, and when she had no money, a share of the crop and two of the kids from the flock. 'But I will let you stay. You will keep the flock for me, and do anything else that I ask. In return you may live here and have what I give you as your portion from the goats and from the land.'

Around him I saw the nods of agreement from the villagers who had gathered, some faces softened with pity for me and for the old woman's death, but many hardened. 'You are a stranger,' their faces said. 'We have no need to take care of you.' And as if the unspoken thought was in the air, he added. 'You came from nowhere. How do we know who you are?' He shrugged. There was little I could say, except agree.

So began the drudgery of life as his worker. Work undertaken with love, and poor food shared in kindness, had salvaged me from the wreck and drowning of my previous life, but without the essence of her goodness I fell again into deep and heavy waters. Waters of loneliness, of a nameless terror that I would never know who I was or where I belonged. Day after day I led the flock up to the hills and watched them, bringing them down at sunset to huddle with them on warmer nights or to secure them within the pen and throw myself on the heap of skins in the corner of her house. I tilled the soil of the patch of earth to sow barley, and tended the two straggling vines. He came to take from me all that I produced and choose the best of the kids for himself and gradually his demands increased: a larger flock of goats to watch, and a herd of pigs grunting and half wild in the lower field. I lost a sense of each day passing, watching only the seasons turn their great wheel of change in the earth and sky. Aware often in the night hours that the gulf between my feeling self, enduring the hunger and hardship of this life, and the far distant watching self, was becoming wide and fixed and that I might awake and find no bridge between the two. I feared yet longed for escape into the flight of what I knew was madness. I gripped reality with rituals of counting and rhymes of memory, numbering and naming the creatures, the trees along the goat trails, the people I passed. They saw me murmuring and muttering to myself, and I saw them avoid my eyes, and even daily greetings ceased.

When it came, it overtook me with a roar as of thunder, a storm, a drenching of mind. Yet on a clear day, a day of intense sun and heat, when suddenly, as noon pressed down on me like a slab of stone so that I was gasping and sick under its weight, the sky split open and through it poured all the birds of the heavens, shrieking and cawing, and each of them taking away a piece of myself, little pieces of my mind. I ran, I remember now, screaming from the hillside to the house, leaving the flock to itself. When he came to find me I fought him and the crowd that followed him, and they overcame me and tied me up like a dog. I was beaten and left bruised and helpless in the field outside the house, secured with ropes. Somehow I broke free and took to the hills, wandering in solitary places, calling out for help, gashing myself with sharp stones. Sometimes a group from the village would search for me and try to bring me back again with ropes and chains. Perhaps they were afraid that I would attack them while they slept or steal their creatures. I broke free again and again, and found a hiding place among the tombs, the ancient caves where the living and the dead have sheltered. Not alone. Others, outlawed, mad, devil-driven like myself, raging and screaming with the torment of our separation from each other, from ourselves.

Days, months, years perhaps, crawled by. Yet even in this there was kindness. Women from the village would come with food and clothing for us, leaving this on the edge of the Lake for us to take so that we would not starve or go utterly naked. And from a long way away I watched them and understood that it was pity that gave them the courage to pause and look for us before they turned and walked back to their homes.

But today. Today I watched as the squall blew up over the Lake, suddenly, strongly, just as my own storm had raged in my mind, and remembering, I ran to and fro and laughed as the wind carried me, and the rage and destruction blew from me to cause the waves to swamp the little boat out there in the midst of the water. And, just as it started, it ceased. A huge and instant calm, that spread from the boat like oil upon the waves and the wind fading into a whisper. And then you came, helping to pull the boat up the beach, and advancing towards us even though your friends hung back. Men in rags, with bloodied arms and chests from self-wounding and deep sores on wrists and ankles from the ropes and chains. The stench of us, the cries and screams. Some fled, one other I remember stayed near me. You spoke, a clear command cutting through all the mad and demonised outcry of our mouths, and there was silence. The storm passed with the pigs panicking down the ravine into the Lake. Then to me, a question. The same question. 'What is your name?'

I had only the answer that had been given me as they fought to control me and chain me afresh. *He's full of demons this one, mad as hell itself. Legions of devils I call him.* 'Legion,' I answered. 'For I, we, are many.'

I barely noticed what was happening around me. The swineherds fleeing screaming to tell the village of what was happening. The hesitation of your friends as you sent for the cushion from the stern of the boat to rest my body on and stripped off your outer cloak to wrap around me. Water was brought and with it you bathed the filth from me, even my matted and stinking hair and beard. You took wine and oil from the pack one of them carried, and dressed each wound and sore, to cleanse and soothe. Familiar, healing movements. And all the time you talked, gently, rebuilding my mind, putting together its fragments.

'The storm,' I muttered, shamed, still in the half-way land between madness and sanity. 'I sent it to destroy you.'

'No, no,' you said laughing. 'You had no power to do that. I was asleep when it started, and I was dreaming of you, and of you being whole again. I came here for you.'

And later you said, 'I will give you a new name.' Then you whispered, to me alone, 'Your new name is Philo, friend, and you will find friends and family as you return to your village.'

'But may I not come with you?' I cried, terrified for a moment that I would be alone again, and all that had been mended would crack apart and I would lose myself.

'No, go back to your village and tell them what I have done. They will listen to you, and I promise all will be well with you. There will come a time when you will hear of me again. Wait for news from Jerusalem.'

Clothed, calm, whole in my mind, I watched you turn back to the boat, your friends half-kind as they caught my eyes, half shame-faced in their hurry to leave such desolation. Outraged villagers were now hurrying to the scene. Angry, but awed at what they saw, the crowd urged you to leave, yet strangely made room for me and for the other man you had healed and restored. Perhaps they saw men who had in some miraculous way been touched by the power of the heavens. Perhaps that which was most human within them had been moved with pity. I stood with them, close to a man I recognised as the elder of the village and his wife, who put his hand upon my shoulder in welcome and acceptance. Together we watched you and your friends push the boat out into gentle surf and row out into the Lake, raising the single sail to catch the wind and cross over to the western shore. And then I turned and walked with them, towards what has become my home.

I Will Repay

A hideous death. My sister's son. Close kin. The last one left of all our hopes.

I think of him, led out among his accusers, and the loneliness of that final staggering thrust that left him helpless as they hurled down rocks, bruising and bloodying him and breaking open the precious casket of the head. They were not men who did this, each mindful of their own humanity and hesitant to break another's open. They were a pack of dogs, baying and screaming curses, and their religious leaders stood apart lest blood should spatter them into uncleanness. But blessing them with orthodoxy just the same. According to the Law.

Perhaps it is a way to give each man a choice, to say you too are linked to this judgement, this life, this death. Your hand is part of this, as truly as if it held a sword or loosed an arrow. And that might hold a man back, remind him of the terror of that act. The fragile link of shared flesh between man and man, man and woman, might leap between the victim and the executioner and cry out, mercy. But it did not.

So I have twisted in mind and body through sleepless nights since the news reached us from the south. And despite the comfort of the brotherhood we share here, and all their gentle arguments to seek peace, to show mercy, I struggle daily with the seething rage I feel, and the horror of it all.

He had gone to visit family in Jerusalem, taking gifts from our community to help them through these times of hardship. Their lives—all our lives—had been turned upside down following those heady days of Pentecost. A faith that shimmered with light and hope. The shared food, the generous openness to one another, the strong and close certainty of a resurrected Master. But then the growing number of those who vanished, in the hours before dawn, to the deeper darkness of prison. Show trials, sudden judgements, beatings and executions. And such courage, such comradeship! We sent Nathan to take them gifts and speak encouragement, and the Temple police came for him. A neighbour had betrayed them. All the household, men and women and children, gone with him, first to prison, then to the quarry for stoning.

He was the last of our family: my wife and I childless, and she dead long ago. My sister's son. And so you say to me, and I hear it now, droning within my head, 'Forgive, forgive. Be at peace'. In the daytime you sit beside me and show pity for the tears of a man aged suddenly into weakness. And at night that other voice, a voice I cannot bear to hear, 'Forgive, forgive. Trust again'.

But I cannot.

Now the news comes. Breathlessly riding in, to warn us ahead of that group of zealots commissioned to seek out the community here and lead it to judgement. The religious police. On the road to Damascus. And I am pacing to and fro on the roof churning the news in my mind: and its taste is like bile in the mouth.

We wait. Some send wives and children into the villages for safety. But I have nothing to lose here now, though fear and hate grip me, and the faith I thought so real that I could lean upon it like a rock has fallen away from me.

Scrambling footsteps on the stairs, and news close to madness. A jolt of lightning, unbearable to the eyes. A man toppled from his horse and led blind into the city. So we wait.

And now the unspeakable call: 'You go. Touch him, bring him back into humanity again.'

I cannot go. Do you not know what he has done? Men, women and children imprisoned, stoned, tormented? How can I go and touch a man whose hands are stained with the blood of my own sister's son? Who has come here to drag us to prison and to death? I cannot, will not, go.

'He is asking for you. Three days in a tomb of blind darkness. He too is filled with terror and the horror of what he has done. I have shown you to him, and he knows the cost of this to you. The first words he hears now will mark his life forever. He will carry my Words beyond your imagining to the edge of the Empire.'

And I am silent. Rage, vengeance, hatred swoop through me like a descent of vultures.

'What do you want, Ananias? An eye for an eye, broken bone for bone, beating for beating, death for death? I can promise you that he will suffer imprisonment, pain and death for me. Will that compensate you for your loss? Is it vengeance that you want? Is it still the Law that rules you? Or mercy?'

While he waits in the prison of his blindness, I wrestle like Jacob with an impossible adversary, and shiver in the heat of the sun.

My sandals scuff the dust as if all other sounds have fallen silent now. I descend the stairs, seeking water to wash away the stain of tears and cleanse my hands before turning from the house to Straight Street. A short journey, but it is all of my life.

I linger at the threshold of his shadowed room before entering. A small man, helpless, groping towards me as I step into his darkness.

'Brother Saul,' I say, and the words choke with bitter phlegm. 'Brother Saul.'

And then that murmur within me, 'This is your inheritance. This is your heir.'

Then I lean forward to take the trembling hands in my own and weep as he is healed.

Mirage

Stories blow along the ancient travellers' routes like uprooted bushes in the desert, like dust clouds that spiral and dance in gusts of sharp, hot, snapping wind. Or they hover like mirages, full of promise and illusion, beckoning forward to nothing. To a place of no-arrival.

But there was a story once, and it has grown in the telling, passing from traveller to traveller, shifting its shape and meaning: there was a story once, and I was part of it, following a mirage, tugged by the desert wind. Nearly a life-time ago, but I remember more now, and understand a little, and it seems right to tell of it and give it place and time before the story whisks away into legend or becomes like the tales we tell to children, and loses all its truth.

You would not recognise me. Not then. You see me now in the consulting room, or in the hours of pain and fear when you call for me, and I move to reassure, to diagnose, to treat whenever possible. To touch, to establish that bond of unspoken kinship to you, to take the dread of pain and death into myself and hold it if I can. I learned those things. That touch is more than words. That the eyes speak more than the voice. That the body is a marvellous thing that heals itself in almost every situation. Until a whisper of mortality slips into the ears of the soul, and takes up its hiding place there. I learned those things, watching, serving, holding, long before I trained for medicine. I learned them as I saw the sickness grow in him and the spirit of the man burn as he fought to make the long journey, consuming energy, life itself, as he travelled.

I was fifteen. A time when everything is observed with fierce concentration, and felt with the sharpness of anguish, the simplicity of devotion. My mother and I had been born into his service, and when he was insistent that he must go, must carry the frailty of himself on this search, I went with him. I could care for the animals and secure places for us to stay. And more, I could nurse him and give him the care that he needed and keep hidden from the prying eyes of other travellers the desperate nature of his need. My mother showed me the measure of opium to give him when the pain became excruciating. She spoke with me of the needs that might come, to wash him, to enable him to relieve himself, to find food that might be digestible, to make sure that there was always water or water mixed with wine. And in telling me, she wept, for he was loved and honoured, and she knew he would not return. Before we left he handed us both the documents that gave us freedom and more than enough financial provision to make a home and livelihood. What I did not know then was that he had set up a fund for me to gain a training, for he had already ensured that I could read and write. So I could be a lawyer or a doctor, a banker or an engineer. The stigma of slavery utterly gone.

'We go first to meet old friends,' he said, shaking out the reins of his horse and smiling for a moment without a shadow of pain or age. 'Friends I studied with, long ago. Letters have come and gone between us all this time, but we have not met in thirty years. But now. Now.' And his thoughts drifted away from me into some mystery, some memory perhaps that I could not follow, and then he smiled and with an energy I had never seen, touched his heels to his horse's flanks and moved ahead of me to the town gate and the beginning of the trade route West.

We kept to clear tracks across the barren country, following in the dust of other travellers, the slots of hooves and wheels, but keeping separate. Not aloof: he was not a proud man, but separate, conserving energy, hiding the grey sweat of pain, the slumped weariness at the end of each day. At nightfall, I found us lodgings, brought him food and drink, then slept outside his door, or with the animals—his horse and mine and the mule that carried the burden of our clothes and necessaries. So we journeyed. A good day would take us forward twenty miles. Some days five, and then sweating and crumpled over his horse's neck I would bring him to some tent or lodging, desperate to help him from the saddle and settle him to ease the pain. Always the sun burned above us, reaching such a height of power and strength at noon it was as if it pressed us to the ground with a giant's fist. At night, the heat of the day fled away and sheer cold gripped us. The darkness was studded with astonishing stars whose patterns moved ceaselessly, tirelessly, across the dome of the sky.

Many weeks later we came to a city in the haze of early evening, towers and high walls faintly tinged by the pink and orange of a sun that slid reluctantly from the sky. The warmth of the day, held in its stone and dust, the smells of cooking, the raucousness of voices smote us. After the silence, the separateness, it shocked me, though something in my youth longed to explore, to follow the beckoning trails of alleys and run my fingers through the displays of the market—silks and spices and fruits. Now, as at the beginning, I saw a new energy in him, and without hesitation he beckoned me forward to follow him. We rode through a sequence of winding lanes between high white walls until we came to an open courtyard, a fountain playing in a marble pool, scurrying servants coming to us to take the horses, and a shout of welcome from the doorway as though the master of the house had spent his day looking out for us. Jealous, I could not let them help him from his horse, but steadied him until he was able to stand and move forward to the greeting that awaited him—his host running down the steps to him and they embraced and kissed and wept like brothers.

He knew. He turned and saw me clutching the reins of the mule, my face stubborn, and called me over. 'My faithful Azir,' he said, gently. 'He has been like a son to me on this long journey.' Then his face lost all colour, and as he fell we caught him and carried him into the house and to his room.

All that night he slept fitfully and I watched him and wiped his forehead, giving him water mixed with wine to sip whenever he woke. I fell asleep as dawn's promise crept into the high window above his head, then jolted awake as he stirred and smiled, his eyes full of youth again despite the wretchedness of his body. Food and drink were brought and he was able to wash and dress and stand unsupported.

As we left his bedchamber we found his friend pacing the corridor, and again, that eagerness, that comradeship, revived him. 'Come with me,' he said, and leant on my arm and we walked down the long marble hall to the courtyard and he sat with his friend talking.

Old stories, old laughter, and then, suddenly, the conversation turned. Turned to a gravity and complexity that I could not follow, and by that time my eyes were heavy with the sleep lost in the night, and with the many nights that had preceded it. I found myself nodding forward, catching fragments only of talk that seemed to be of calculations, times and distances, with charts of huge patterns spread upon the low table. Suddenly, the clatter of hooves at the gateway and an urgent, demanding voice, swift steps across the courtyard and a messenger carrying a scroll. My master's friend rose to his full height, broke the seals and read the message, turning rapidly to excuse himself, and then to summon horse and give instructions for the care of his guests. 'I will return this evening, I trust,' he said. 'And we should soon be joined by our third friend of those student days! He has travelled the Silk Road from the East, but I have news from him that he will be with us before nightfall. If I am delayed, you will have much to share.' Then he walked quickly to the gate, mounted the horse held ready for him and rode away.

'He is the King's chief advisor,' I learned. 'Such a summons must be obeyed, most especially now if he is to have leave for the long journey that awaits us.' So I waited, and my master rested in the shade, and the day moved over the courtyard in shortening and lengthening blue-black shadows. As I waited, I pondered: this unknown journey; these friends; their talk, so hard to follow, of the movements of the stars, the geometry of the Greeks, the learning and debate of Alexandria. Then, towards evening, a third traveller, thin and sparse, with deep eyes that read you as he greeted you. And our host returned, weary with responsibilities, and we ate together and the talk strayed through Greek to Aramaic languages and Latin, with laughter and memories, but with an increasing sense of an approaching climax as the meal ended.

'Now,' said our host, and beckoned us up the winding stairway to a high tower where, in the deepening indigo of night, a million stars waited for us, forming themselves into patterns and constellations that these men traced with eager, sweeping arms. Dreamers, wide eyed and passionate, yet serious in their calculations and their careful measuring instruments, leaning up against the balustrade to point and gesticulate.

'It was always you,' they said, half laughing, yet tender in their recollections and in their gestures of affection for him as they turned to my master. 'You saw the patterns long ago, and the converging pathways of the stars. And now the time has come.'

'And we must begin our journey, as soon as we are packed and ready,' he answered them. He held my arm closely as we descended the stairs. 'Tomorrow, we ride west and then south by the old merchants' road. I will need your help to pack, and all your care if I am to travel.' I saw his friends' deep concern as they marked his weakness, the greyness that invaded his face and broke in sweat on his forehead. 'Azir is a son to me,' he said to them. 'He will help me reach our destination. I cannot manage without him.' And he smiled at me even though he was trembling with weakness and in much pain.

And so we rode out, in opal light that flowed from the sky as dawn broke, giving ourselves several hours of coolness before the smiting sun forced us to seek refuge. Very little baggage, strapped on horses and the mule, and dull, inconspicuous clothing. Slowly, I came to know and understand a little of my master's friends. I served them all, finding lodging, tending and guarding the animals. The cares of royalty, the burden of his responsibilities, still hung on the first of them. The lines around his mouth and eyes seemed grained with responsibility, his voice strong with a readiness to command, yet always gentle, always courteous to me. The second, whom I had barely met before we set off, was quiet. No, quiet is not enough to describe him. He held silence within himself as though he were a cup, a chalice of stillness. Late into the night under the stars, and sometimes early even before the dawn I saw him leave the room or the tent where we lodged, and pace beneath the dark sky. I watched him once, until I realised that this was too private, too costly for me to see. Sometimes his arms were lifted up as though in prayer or entreaty, or his hands clenched with some great struggle. And there were times when I was tending to my master as he returned, bending his head under the lintel of the door, or stooping at the tent's entrance, and in the faint light I sometimes saw the track of tears on his cheeks and glistening in his beard.

They spoke little, as though their agreement was so deep it needed few words. I came to understand the need for haste, the need for secrecy. I saw that their journey was the coming together of long roads, separated for a lifetime until they felt this compulsion, this certain knowledge. A compulsion that had brought them together at last to search the skies for direction and seek with the passion of their youth, the dedication of their age, the One foretold. So much I understood, and gave myself to serve them as they travelled, to make it possible, I told myself, for my master to succeed in his quest, at whatever cost. And gradually I learned from them how to read the skies and recognise the burning conjunction of stars that called them forward.

And so we came at last, and after many weeks, to the weary, indifferent guards of the border crossing and then to Jerusalem. And here they sought out a place to stay and brought from their packs the clothes of their rank and dignity to dress to greet the King. I waited whilst they sought their royal audience, standing in the market place whilst soldiers thrust their way through the crowd, merchants called their wares, blind beggars whimpered as they were shoved to the edge, religious leaders drew aside from the women and the urchins of the streets. Once again the magic of the city, the juxtaposed glamour and wretchedness, the dazzle of goods and trades took hold of my youth, even though I felt weighted with the solemnity of the quest.

It was many hours before they returned, but then, hurriedly, reproaching themselves as fools to have looked in the Palace of such a man for the One they sought. And in their haste there was urgency, even a sense of danger, my master finding within himself an extraordinary strength. They changed their clothes, and we rode out quickly and left the city through the South Gate, taking the roads through the hill country. And all night they pointed to that dazzling configuration in the heavens. Until and at last, they came very early the next day to Bethlehem, a straggling village, hardly a town, of white houses, goats and donkeys tethered at gate posts and olive trees grey-green in the fields. Quiet under the open sky.

Here they seemed to need no guidance, dismounting before a small house, flat-roofed, humble, even poor. I stood, holding the reins, perplexed, whilst they sought in their packs for gifts concealed all this while and never spoken of. My master turned: 'Come. Come with me now. I need your arm. This has been your journey also.' So I looped the reins together hurriedly. Then they knocked on the simple door, and each one, bowing his head beneath the crossbeam, entered. And I with them.

What can I tell you? There was nothing extraordinary there, yet everything. A young woman, hardly older than I; a man, stooping protectively over her. At her breast, covered hastily with a linen cloth, a baby. She turned to see us as we entered, and brought the baby onto her lap and murmured to her husband as the three old men knelt down before her and her child. The baby, scarcely six weeks old, I think, opened the clear liquid unfocused eyes of babyhood and seemed to gaze at them. There were no words spoken, no movement, not at first. I too knelt at the heels of my masters, and watched, sensing mysteries that I could not grasp, not then. And only now, a little. Beneath her eyes, the blue-black semi-circles of sleeplessness, and gauntness in the cheeks, but the curve of her mouth was full of tender pride. Her husband's arm encircled her. Square strong craftsman's hands. A serious, steady face of great kindness. Around them, a home of extreme simplicity with meagre furniture, a bed with rugs in the corner, a hearth and cooking pots, shelves, benches.

Then there were words and explanations, phrases of Aramaic that I could barely follow. Their quest. The folly of their visit to Jerusalem The One, they said, born King of the Jews. Their recognition of his kingship even in his babyhood. The great patterns of the stars that had brought them here.

But it is this that stays with me.

They brought out their gifts as they spoke, and one by one offered them to the child as he lay in her lap. The one whom I had come to know as Balthazar, the king's advisor, held out a simple circlet of gold, the crown of a prince I would imagine, though I had never seen such a thing. The dark eyes of the baby mirrored it in the oil-lamp's light and he reached out wandering hands and arms to take it as it was offered, holding its sullen, gleaming, weighty smoothness and pulling it towards himself, until it rested on his shoulder.

Then Gaspar drew out the casket he had brought and opened its lid, and the heady fragrance of Frankincense resin breathed out into the little room, and he too, leant forward to let the baby touch the gift. The child's mother smiled and gently took the weight of the gold circle from his shoulder to where it could rest alongside him in her lap as the uncertain, wavering hands of the baby reached for the casket and the old man, weeping, held its weight. And the child brought it to his own little chest, above the heart, and held it there, serene and still for many moments.

Then Melchior, my own master, brought his gift, a precious flask of alabaster, sealed at the neck, made I guessed then, to hold the oils for anointing at burial, Myrrh among them. The alabaster whiteness gleamed in his dark hands, and I marked even at that moment, their fragility and trembling. And as he approached the baby, the child's hands took, not the flask, but his hands, and brought them to his face, his eyes steadfast, drinking, it seemed to me, the face and form of my master as though some strange process of understanding passed between them. Some absorption of his pain and frailty, his mortality, into himself.

We stayed in stillness for a long time. Then the young husband stirred, spoke gently to his wife, and offered bread and wine, olives and figs for our refreshment. Three old men moved stiffly from their knees and we ate and drank in their home, grateful for their kindness. And it seemed that we returned to reality, if reality is what we call it. Until we entered the house I had considered all this journey an old man's quest, a mirage of their youth, but I had seen into the truths that lie at the heart of dreams and desires, here in this humble home, and in the wandering hands and eyes of a tiny baby. I had seen these men, amongst the wisest of their generation, give the gift of their lives to this child. Even now, I wonder at it.

We left in the cool of the evening, seeking to stay at the inn, but in the early hours of the morning the lord Gaspar roused us to tell us of his dream, a warning that King Herod would seek our lives and we must not return to the court of Jerusalem. So we did not take the expected route, but rode west to the coast, taking ship at Joppa and setting out for Alexandria. And there on board ship, my master

Melchior lay resting against my shoulder under an awning on deck, his eyes gazing out to the horizon. 'Tell your mother,' he said, 'that I am going home by another way.' Then he thanked me, and said farewell to his friends, and shuddered once, and smiled and died.

After we landed at Alexandria, we parted. I took the long road home, selling the horse and riding the mule. 'When the time is right,' Balthazar had said to me, 'come to me and I will enable you to train as a doctor.' For I had already spoken of my desire.

So it was, seven years later, that I returned to the city of white walls and the marble courtyard. Since then, I have found myself waiting always for news from Jerusalem. It is more than thirty years since we followed the dream across the desert roads from the east. It is only now, as I tell you, that I know the certainty of its enduring substance.

Loosing the Cords of Orion

Under a sky lavish with stars two old men rested, at ease together after shared food. Bread and rough wine, herb-flavoured meat and dates and raisins had been served. The women now withdrew. Their voices carried on the light wind, animated with news and compared stories. The older man smiled and his hands encircled the wooden cup, turning it gently to feel the carving of bird and beast under his fingers. 'So,' he said. 'It is good to hear them laugh. To make friends, to hear news, to weave a little history together. We do not often travel so far nowadays.' The southern road joined the eastern trade route here and there was shade and greenness, water for their animals, a sanctuary on the very brink of the desert.

As the sun fell suddenly below the edge of the hills the men sensed the long sigh from the ever-moving sand. The heat exhaled and the dark and chill fell together. They felt the minute grain and grit of the sand, running in shivers of air towards their tents and gritting their necks and faces where the sweat lingered. In silence, they gazed out over a vast landscape that lingered gold for seconds at its very edge in the last flare of the setting sun, and then watched the sky turn from turquoise to sapphire and the clustering, crowding stars rush into their places in the ageless constellations.

'The countless stars,' said the other man, younger perhaps by a decade, though it would be hard to judge the age of either. 'Strange that we seek to find patterns and groupings for them, to make some kind of order in the vastness of it all.' He laughed gently. 'Can you bind the beautiful Pleiades? Can you loose the cords of

Orion? Can you bring forth the constellations in their seasons?' Leaning forward, he looked respectfully at the older man before him. His gaze met and was held by the other's eyes. Each searched the other's face, reading the record of the journey, of distances travelled and endured.

'Tell me, my friend,' said the elder, at length.

'I came seeking you,' he said simply. 'You know how news flows on the desert roads and after months, years maybe, you learn the story of a man who becomes a legend even in his life time. It was your story, or part of it, that I heard, and I knew that we were sharing the same mystery. The same search. The pain and terror as well as the amazing vision.' He stared out to a horizon beyond imagining, glimpsed now in soaring ranges of curves, convex and concave, outlined against the sky. 'All of my life I have been a searcher after God. Men around me spoke of a god who cared for their tribe or territory, or of many gods who must be placated by sacrifice to safeguard the crops and flocks or to provide good weather. I looked into the heavens and the earth and knew that everything in creation must belong to one god alone. And I was certain that he must require righteous conduct and compassion for the poor. I sought to deal justly with my tenants and workers. I watched over my family like a priest. I dared to believe that I walked in his favour and even might trust his friendship.' He paused. 'I do not tell you this to justify myself, but to explain.'

'I understand what you say,' the old man said. 'For me it was one day of compelling truth after months, years, of questions and searching. I must leave everything that was familiar and set out for an unknown land. That in itself was terrifying, a great risk, to cross borders into new territory. I too believed that this god who spoke to me must be the God of the whole earth. I also looked up at the stars to confirm his character and his promise—that I would have descendants as many as those stars that we see pulsing above our heads. And yet for years that promise was not only unfulfilled, but cruel. My wife, beloved as she was, was barren. The journey was not only one of miles but of years. Waiting, being tested, failing often, struggling to know and believe not only the commands of a God who is lord of heaven and earth, but to ask, *Who are you? What kind of God are you?* I stood before him demanding mercy even for the city of Sodom. *Shall not the Judge of the whole earth do right?'*

The older man ceased and for a while they both stayed silent. The wind was stirring now and they drew their cloaks closer. In the distance the jackals were yapping and screeching, and nearer to them, night insects scratched and rustled. 'Tell me more, my brother,' he asked, with great gentleness.

'A day of disaster,' the other man said, simply. For many heartbeats he waited, gathering the strength to overcome the tears and the tightness of throat that came with memory of that day. 'My children, dead. Flocks, herds, servants, all taken from me in that day. I remember crying out, *Why was I ever born? Why did I ever know blessing if it can turn to such agony of soul?* And then my own body, covered with sores, disgusting to myself and others. Even my wife urged me to turn from God and seek death. Men who had shown me respect as a city elder averted their eyes, and I sat outside the town in the dust and in my despair. There was nothing left.'

He turned to the older man, who reached out a hand of great tenderness to touch him, stretching across the years to that unbearable place of memory and healing it.

'Then friends came, men whom I trusted, men with whom I had shared the great hope I had of a God of compassion and justice. They stayed with me in my sorrow and I was glad of their kindness, until they began to speak. Everything they said increased my despair. *He is righteous, blessing the righteous and punishing the guilty. Your suffering proves that you must have sinned against him. You cannot claim to be innocent: your suffering is proof of your guilt. You cannot demand reasons of God.* I began to argue, convinced that in all my ways I had sought to please God, to show compassion to the poor. Their reasoning, their hardness of heart could not be the truth. Could not be the final answer.' The words of his remembered pain hung rigid in the air between them.

'I too came to a place where there were no answers. Nothing that I could understand,' said Abraham, stirring after many moments. 'The long-desired son was born—we called him Laughter for the joy he brought us—and I thought I could see my inheritance stretching out like the stars in the sky, the sand on the seashore. Then one day, the voice spoke, *Take your beloved son Laughter and offer him to me as a sacrifice.* There was nothing I could do but trust, beyond what I could see, in the God I thought I had known.'

The other nodded. 'There is nothing. All that you thought was true in your experience, all your certainties, crumble to ruin. You are right: I knew in my soul that God was still God, the object of all my hope, and that even if he were to slay me I would trust in him. I raged and argued and heard myself crying out for an intermediary, for someone who has eyes of flesh, who feels as we feel, struggles as we struggle. Someone who would plead with God for me as a friend pleads for his friend.'

'For us both,' said the older man. 'To plead for us both.' Again, silence, and around them the desert drew breath and waited.

'How did your story end? For your son is with you, and your tents are filled with laughter again.'

'I took him, with ropes to bind him and wood bundled on the donkey. Weeping, struggling to hide from him what I was commanded to do. At the top of the mountain that voice again: *Don't touch him! Because you were ready to sacrifice him, your beloved son, I know your faith. I will bless you with descendants like the stars and the sand, and all people on earth will be blessed through you.* It was more than my obedience. I glimpsed something beyond what was happening in that hour, on that terrible mountain. He was brought back from the dead. I knew there was a great compassion in that moment for how I felt, the father asked to slay his son. I saw beyond. An understanding beyond the present. That is all I can say.'

As if to himself, the listener said, 'He knows the journey that your feet have taken; he has refined you to prove that you are gold.'

Now, it was good to be silent, men able to share at last the journey of their faith and find rest in each other's company and understanding. The cooking fires were dying down and the chill of night would soon drive them to seek warmth and sleep. Above them the sky had deepened to black and the stars had moved steadily in their ordered and patterned steps towards the horizon. Orion strode forth, the hunter of the heavens, held in the golden links of the constellations.

'And you, Job, my brother?'

'I had my answers—no, not the reasons for my sufferings and loss. But he called to me, awesome, terrifying at first, but commanding me to stand up like a man and speak with him. And even in my grief I felt a kind of laughter in the midst of it all, for what he showed me was the huge wonder of his creation, his care for each creature and knowledge of it—detailed, loving, even playful, as though the great animals cause him to smile with pleasure. The power of storms, the restraint of the sea, all of these things he shared with me, taking me to the dawn of creation when the morning stars sang for joy—these stars that we see gathering in the east. No answers. But I had been heard, and I saw him. I fell down in worship, and in that moment he spoke to my friends. *You have not been speaking the truth about me. My servant Job has spoken what is right about me. He will pray for you and you will be forgiven.* All of my angry questioning, heard and approved—as if I were part of a great council of unseen elders, debating the same question, why do the innocent suffer? He said it again, *My servant Job has spoken what is right about me.* Has God a heart like a man's heart, and does he see with our eyes? Is there a great debate even within the mind of God himself? Does he argue our case before himself and pray for us as he told me to pray for my friends? I, too, in that strange moment, saw beyond my day and beyond my understanding.'

Both men gathered their garments and rose, turning east to see the faint fore-dawn lightening of the sky and embraced, holding each other's shoulders closely and for a long moment, like brothers greeting one another after some timeless voyage across a deep sea.

'Come, my dear friend,' said the older man. 'Let us rest now. Tomorrow I will ask you about your family, your daughters and your sons, the restoration that I see has happened for you. I feel we stand together at the very edge of his ways, hearing a whisper of the truth, trembling at the glimpse we have of what may come.'

After Forty Years

So, I have returned. The end and the beginning join together here, now. That raw recruit, blistered from training camp and the forced march from the port. The veteran due to take a pension and settle—where? I do not know. So many years lie between those two soldiers, so long a time, so great a distance, that I can hardly recognise them both as myself. Only the place remains.

Memory jolts backward to see him then, to smell his sweat, to feel his queasiness after the voyage, his ears jarred with sounds. The stamp of booted feet; the slap of hand to weapon; the raucous chants of song and curse as the company moves up through the winding streets away from the docks; the rasping rise and fall of his breath. His fears of stumbling out of rhythm in the drill, or facing exposure for brass unpolished, leather dulled. The thousand insecurities of a posting abroad. Untried. Unskilled. Eighteen years old.

Since then, years of soldiering and peace-keeping in dusty corners of the world, where languages fall strangely on the ear, formed of breath, or liquid like water, not like my familiar harsh consonants of tongue and teeth. Decades spent stamping down uprisings, policing riots, building roads and bridges. The routines of barrack life, the boredom, the easy comradeship of shared drinking; the terrible loneliness of danger. Miles tramped on rough and broken roads. I struggled then: now I can march twenty miles in the day and think nothing of it. A lifetime.

The road swings up through the same hills. And I find that their shapes are scraped on the back of my eyes like no other, and the smouldering scent of a sun-burnt land and the crushed fragrances of herb sting in my nostrils again. A long march, and time to remember as the afternoon sun stretches our shadows beside us. That boy, hungry for manhood, paces beside me, refusing to remember his mother's tears of farewell and his father's indifferent shrug. In all the years since, he never knew when she died, or if she got the one greasy letter sent in those first days of embarkation. His pack weighs heavy, burdened with gear and weapons on thin shoulders, and with the secret load of fear. Mine, too, is heavy, though the familiar weight is easy, but the scent and sight of this place stirs too much that I have chosen to forget and it clamps down on me, tightening its straps around my chest and heart.

Those early days are a rush and blur of duties and commands for all recruits, but in a strange city, a strange country, they overwhelm you. The people lower their eyes so that you cannot see the hostility in their flickering glances. Their talk is pitched in tones and sounds you do not recognise and the streets are full of strident cries and jostling crowds. You learn to shove and curse through them and feel brutality rise up in you to mask whatever may be vulnerable in yourself. A uniform, a blow, a shout, do not need an interpreter to clear the way, and so you learn quickly. Within a few days the army breaks you in, hardens you, so that you can be sent on any duty without disgracing yourself or your unit with weakness. They choose a tough assignment, and send along a couple of raw youngsters with a squad of old hands to learn the realities of soldiering.

For me, two weeks into my first posting, it was the guard duty at an execution. Brutal, public warnings of the punishment meted out for crime or insurrection. The stench of blood under a ruthless blazing sky, the cries torn out of men who writhed with the slowness of their dying. A jeering crowd. Silent, anguished women. I remember how I turned to vomit behind a thorn bush, sickened with the horror of it, desperate to escape the scorn of my comrades. And as I turned back, wiping my sour mouth, I saw the man's eyes. Watching me with an expression I could not read, could not understand. Kindness? Pity? Calmness in his eyes, despite the rictus of pain twisting his face.

A day of unendurable length, ending in darkness and the broken indignities of slung bodies and burials, and a guard duty over. My shoulders slapped with rough sympathy by an older soldier, and I stumbled away to seek my manhood among the girls that hung around the bars. I chose one in the flickering light because it seemed to me that she still knew how to smile with her eyes not just her mouth, even though she called me 'soldier boy' and pulled me down to her with practised arms and hands that stripped off belt and webbing with accustomed skill. I took her then and sought her for days and nights afterwards like a draught of forgetfulness, night after night in the dark passageways, and against stones still hot from the day's sun; gritty, sweating, urgent. Until one day she told me. Perhaps it was mine. I would have killed any other man who touched her. Stupid with drink and longing, homesick fool, I said, 'Then marry me.' We had some mumbling civil ceremony and set up quarters in the shadow of the barracks. I scrambled every morning to be on parade, leaving her tumbled on the bed, the place messed with food and dishes, clothes, the slow encroachment of dirt and disorder. When the baby came, it was a son. She was so warmed and glowing with her love for him, and mine for both of them, that it was as though a lamp was lighted in a place of shadows. That was before bitterness crept back into the room like cockroaches.

Six months after his birth, the army sent me north on a fresh tour of duty. There were cries of separation, promises meant and never kept and a swirl of dust from marching feet and the churning wheels of transport coming between me and the glimpse I had of her, the boy in her arms, waving. I sent my pay and letters, and messages for the boy, imagining him growing. I counted the days to my return on leave to play with him and teach him the half-remembered games and rhymes of my own boyhood. In my night time dreams he grew and strengthened, fathered as I never was. But in the stark daylight we put down skirmishes in the hill country, with more blood, more summary executions, crushing riots, breaking apart families and villages, leaving our trail of conquest written in the dust behind us. Then, six months later, the messages from her faded away, and one day mine returned to me, 'Not Known'. And so I lost my son.

I sent messages, word of mouth, scribbled letters with each and every comrade posted there and to those I knew still stationed in the city garrison. But no response from her, only a vague rumour that she had fled north-west with the boy, and after the year passed, and I was sent to peacekeeping duties in Europe, I gave way to despair and hardened myself to soldiering and to the brief, intense distractions that come with the job. There are no excuses: I am only saying what was, what is, the reality. I was posted hundreds of miles away, and under a different sky, and in the hubbub of different voices and commands and duties, I lost him, and I lost her, forever.

But now I march again, through these foothills, towards the ring of mountains that surround the city. After forty years the memories I had dulled, suppressing into indifference, twist now at my heart, raw, snatching breath, as they did then. O my son, my son, my feet tramp out as we swing steadily up the gradient, through the abandoned olive groves and the ransacked farms. As we halt for minutes to drink, to check the final orders, the stench reaches us. Burning, stale and pungent; the very odour of death and destruction. I have smelt before the stink of ruined villages and massacre, but not this. Not this desolation, not the ruin of a city. The marble facades that caught the sun and dazzled the eye are fragments that we crush underfoot as we move into unrecognisable streets and squares to relieve the garrison, consolidate the conquest. Gutted women, unburied. Children sprawled in angles of lifeless legs and arms like grasshoppers. Birds that fly away slowly, insolently, from the bodies they scavenge. Flickering at the corner of my eye, other children flash like lizards in corners of walls and tottering doorways, too afraid to beg. O my son, my son.

Later, that evening, my round of duties done, I climb alone above the valley where the city rubbish burned—though all the city is rubbish now, and still smouldering and stinking—to the place where all those years ago I saw a man endure the unendurable and yet show kindness to a shamed and trembling young man, vomiting into a thorn thicket. His look has never left me, even in my desperation to forget the horror and stifle any humanity that might betray my weakness. I remember the tone of the voice of the officer of the guard: 'God, God!' he said, awed at the man's dignity. I was too young, too uncertain of myself to offer such respect: I could only flee and hide myself in her flesh.

And now, I stand here more alone than I have ever felt. Within weeks my service ends, and I take a pension and buy a small farm or a wine shop maybe, somewhere, for I have no roots. And as I turn, seeking a fresh wind from the hills to take the foetid stink of death from me, the half-crazed resolution grows in me, to search for my son, to find her if she still lives. To build again, to heal the wounds, to meet the sons and daughters of my son, and his grandchildren, for if he lived, after forty years, there will be family. There have been rumours too, mocked among soldiers, of the man who died on this grim hillside, and the followers who kept his name alive. That too, I can search out. Perhaps my son has taken my name, or perhaps she hid his birth. But her name I know: Tabitha, and it may be that she found refuge in a town or village north of here. That at least I might discover. And if all else fails, and there is no substance to these dreams, I will seek out one of these desolate children of the ruins and give him a home and livelihood. And so begin again.

A Flight of Doves

I learned to run away as soon as I learned to push one foot in front of the other. Seizing my small sister by the hand or arm or wrist, and half-carrying her because her tottering legs could hardly walk. We would stumble, gasping and sobbing into the shelter of the tree and hide there, pressed against its trunk, waiting for the kindness of silence. Then we would slide home as the shadows moved and stretched across the yard, pausing at its edge and waiting until our mother came, calling gently to us, herself still shaking and pale. We would drink water cool from the well and be hushed and comforted with a handful of raisins. And the man would have tramped away into the hills, matching his rage against the rigid strength of the rocks and the awful emptiness of the wilderness.

His anger terrified us. It fell like a fist on the table, splitting the meal apart. It hurled against us like stones, splinters of rock that gashed us with words. He rarely used violence, but his rage tore at us, wife and children, and tore at himself. He was consumed with judgement. The smallest fault at the meal table, a whisper of defiance, an error in the day's lesson learned brought down his anger, the anger of a man who walked in fear always that he was to be judged by an implacable god. Fear made him a tyrant at home. In the village, he walked alone, men drawing back from the inflexibility of his righteousness. He carried the burden of a prophet. Enraged at the deviations from law and godliness that he saw in the ignorant practices of the people in their worship; consumed with the history of a nation dwindling into apostasy, forgetting its heritage. All around, the alliance and empire-building of neighbouring states threatened the integrity of Israel, and he saw a ruthless balance of faithlessness and destruction, an inevitable end that only a restoration to moral and religious perfection could avert. So, he terrorised us, the miniature nation over which he had control.

When I was born, he was still in years a young man, perhaps no more than thirty, but old and bowed with the burden he carried. As he aged, I saw his burden consume him, turning his hair and beard white, lining his face with inexorable marks of wrath and solitude. Scars made from within. When my mother died soon after my sister's wedding, I ran away. My sister married a pious and gentle man, and I knew her to be safer and happier than she had ever been at home, and so I was free. I stole some money, some clothing, enough food to last me for the journey south, a goatskin full of water mixed with wine, and fled in the early hours of the day before the sun burned.

I did not return for five years. And only then because word reached me through my mother's people that all was changed.

I came slowly over the brow of the hill, alert in every part of my being, like a deer that fears the hunter waiting in the shadow of the tree. I remembered in the sweat of my body and the shivering of my bowels the terror that had driven me from this house. I saw at the gate of the yard a small bowed man, seated on the bench. As I watched, he stooped to scatter seed and doves circled round him and returned again and again to cluster at his feet, before flying to perch on the ridge that ran round the house roof. My mother had loved them, feeding them as they came to her hand, soothed by their crooning. Grief, pity, rage. I do not know which most clenched my breath and caused my eyes to flood with tears that had waited too long.

As my sight sharpened again I saw him turn and raise his hand, shading his eyes to look south against the sun and scan the road. I watched him as he focused and identified me, his hand dropping to his side before he ran clumsily through the gate towards me, his robe flapping against his legs. An old man running up the hill.

And I was rigid in his embrace. The silence waited for words to fill it. What can be said? Cicadas scraped and whirred. Dust resettled around our feet. When he broke the quiet, he spoke only six words: 'My son. My son. Forgive me.' He took my hand and led me down the road, through the familiar yard to the door, and called for water and wine, food and fresh clothes. As the servant bustled, he brought me to a bench in the shade and kneeling, took from me my worn sandals, washing my feet from the jar of water the servant brought him.

Long afterwards, dazed, weary beyond telling, I sat with him and we shared food. I waited for the blessing, drank the wine slowly and ate the meat and the fresh bread. Quietness flowed from him and gathered me like a cloak. Words formed in my mind that I had never spoken willingly: *my Father.* All through the meal, I felt his eyes on me, waiting for some signal, some permission for him to speak. Silence hung awkwardly between us. As darkness fell, and the oil lamps were lit, I was drawn to look at his face, despite myself. The softening light touched him, and yet sharpened the lines set deeply around his eyes and the corners of his mouth. His eyes no longer stabbed and sparked, but held a gentleness that I had never known. Involuntarily, I lifted my hands to break and share the bread. 'I do not understand,' I heard my mouth speak for me.

He talked for many hours that night. My memory is of moments of great clarity and stillness amongst a whirlpool of chaos and mystery. I heard of a man who had walked at the very roots of the mountains and in the ravines of the sea, of primal and inchoate cries of emotion in a place of drowning. A man pursued by the dread of God; a dread so terrible that it tore apart the fanatical construction of his understanding. The terror that an encounter with God would not vindicate his passion for judgement but demolish him with mercy.

He also ran away.

Not long after my mother died, he told me, he walked the hills late into the night feeling over and over, like a stone in his belly, the prophetic burden to go to Nineveh. Not to preach the impending judgement of an awful God against a cruel and wicked people, but to offer them repentance. Weighed down with a word that contradicted everything that gave him meaning, he fled west, taking ship from Joppa to go to Tarshish, on the uttermost edge of the Great Sea. Knowing, as he travelled, that he put himself in the place of judgement and expecting nothing less in the rigid set of weights and balances that formed his mind. Indeed, in some perverse way, welcoming it.

Storms are sudden on the Great Sea, tempestuous and dangerous, and before many days, the ship was plunging and wallowing in enormous waves and the wind had ripped the sails and tackle from the mast. The steersman cried out that he could no longer hold the course and the sailors threw cargo overboard, and crouched wretched and terrified as their ship was thrown down the steep sides of waves to jolt and shudder with the impact. They cried out to their gods to save them. And through it all, he slept. Exhausted with fear and the strain of rebellion, weary of himself, perhaps. More, he came to realise, he was deaf with indifference to their fate, unconscious of their cries for rescue. Without pity, he was oblivious to their condition. When they woke him to join their prayers, he held himself apart. As they cast lots to find the cause of their misfortune, he admitted his guilt. His calmness terrified them. His God was the creator of heaven and earth and the sea and everything in it, he told them. He was running from God, and the fault was his. His iron justice admitted the sin, accepted that his life must now be taken to redress the balance. But even as he stood, detached, stern, unfeeling, there was a part of himself that was awakening. He saw the men struggling to find a way to row back to land without having to destroy him. They cried out to God to forgive them if they took his life. He heard their humanity, even if he did not comprehend it.

As they threw him overboard, the salt and terrible waves overwhelmed him.

Just for a little, he gasped and struggled above the surface, sensing as the ship drew away from him that it moved more surely. But the waves crashed over his head and he fell through huge walls of water into what he described as the very depths of the grave, the thick night of death itself. He touched the profound chasms of the deep, and the source of darkness. Out of his mouth came the cry that all his belief in justice had suppressed: 'Save me, O God.' Incoherent, primal, helpless. 'And then,' he said, with a smile full of wonder, 'God had prepared a fish which swallowed me and carried me to shore.' I gestured disbelief, even contempt for such a story. I had been caught up in the amazement of it all, but this turned the story into a tale for children. 'No,' he answered my unspoken thought. 'No, not what you are thinking. This was no beast like the leviathan that terrified our ancestors, nor am I trying to tell in pictures what happened only in my mind. It was a creature that I can only call a fish, prepared for me—a vessel to carry me in its belly to safety.'

I waited. He got up from the table, animated, pacing the room. It was some time before he spoke again, looking at me very carefully to seek my understanding.

'It was himself,' he said, so quietly that I strained to hear him. 'It was himself. God swallowed me into himself to rescue me, and for three days I listened to the beat of a huge heart and felt the vulnerability of the organs encircling me as a womb covers a child. I could have broken out, punctured the softness of the belly, torn at the covering, but I did not. I lay in a great pulsating darkness, admitting that I had encountered rescue when I had expected destruction. Admitting that I, like those helpless sailors, had cried out for rescue, for mercy.'

I entered with him into the enormity of that discovery: his own mortal frailty, his slow recognition of a God not only merciful—all potentates can offer mercy if it pleases them—but vulnerable. Pondering his words, and the change in the man, I sat in quietness again, but lifted my eyes to his face. Waiting for his voice to lead me.

After three days he told me, the fish brought him to land and spewed him out onto a desolate coast. But he described the contractions of the fish more as the contractions of birth, and it was for him a birth into newness, of awareness of that first and gradually of a new identity. The sun warmed and dried him. Kindly folk, alarmed at the wildness of his appearance but recognising both his need and that he was touched by the gods, fed him and helped him on his journey east to the Assyrian capital. There, wild and unkempt, he called for repentance, warning of the judgement to befall them. And the old prophetic voice roared in him and for a little while he forgot the terrors of the deep and his own cries for help. So when his words brought about a huge fervour of repentance in the city, he turned to God in fury. 'I knew it would be so,' he had raved at God. 'I knew you would show mercy and compassion to these people. I would rather die than see this happen.'

'You see,' he told me, 'I had not learned. I was filled with hatred towards these people, this empire that swallows up nations and threatens Israel, these heartless and cruel people who rip up pregnant women and put children to the sword. I had not looked at myself, at the words that I had spoken day after day to my wife and my children, that had pierced them as surely as any sword. Nor had I realised that all my life's energy had been spent upon the call for judgement and the desire for vengeance—every day the cry: *O that you would slay the wicked*. Day after day I had called upon God for the destruction of those who disobeyed his laws.'

Furious, utterly alone, he went to find a hiding place, again as far from God as possible, east of Nineveh, distancing himself from the Temple in Jerusalem and the nation of Israel, turning from the faith of his people in bitterness. He made a rough shelter from the intense heat, and waited for what he hoped would be the destruction of the city. 'But God,' he told me, and there was a wry smile as he spoke, 'had more. He covered me with the huge leaves of a vine, like a tree. I was cooled, even calmed by its shade, and in some strange way comforted, healed. But the next day, as the sun rose and I would have been glad of its covering, I found that its leaves were already withering and the roots were devoured. The morning brought a scorching east wind, and I grew faint and sick with exposure to the heat. I said to God again, in anger, I would rather die'.

He found it hard to describe to me the conversation, half terrible and half humorous, that ensued between himself and God. Like swirling mist in the mind, he said, or clouds drifting against a high sky. Elusive and full of mystery, yet distinct in meaning. A voice, yet not a voice. Nothing like the heavy stone blocks of words that had weighed on him and scoured his soul with their relentless demands for perfection. These were words and ideas that had no roots in his own thinking or his past. *So, you are angry about the plant, troubled that its life should be cut short and your protection gone? But you did not plant or tend this vine. It grew as a gift to shelter you, to cover you with mercy so that you would not feel the unbearable heat of the pitiless sun and faint under its power. Look at this great city, full of men and women and children and their animals, helpless in their ignorance of what is good and evil, utterly without the knowledge of compassion or justice. Their lives cut short without hope. Do you not see that they also need what I prepared for you: rescue, mercy, protection?*

It was many days before he recovered enough to leave the city and begin the long journey back to Israel. A tired man, weary to the core of his being with the depths of his experience and with regret and loss that he now understood for the first time. Yet lighter of heart too, with a sense of a burden lifted, a path of gentleness opened in his thinking. So he travelled slowly, surprised and grateful for the ordinary kindnesses of people in the poor villages who gave him food and shelter, and the travellers who let him join them and offered him the use of a donkey. These things too he realised, had been provided for him, and he recognised the grace of it all, and the bond that links man and man in the fellowship of shared experience.

So he came home, seeing from a distance, the roof of the small farm, the courtyard with its tree of shelter. And here, in his telling, he faltered, and wept. 'Your sister,' he said. 'There in the courtyard, holding out her hands to the doves. She and her husband had cared for the animals and sowed the west field in readiness for my return. Each day they spent time here, just waiting, so that I would not return to emptiness.'

I stood up, locked in myself, moved beyond words, but helpless to express that to him. My hands, clumsy and unpractised, reached to him and held his hands. Even as a child, I had no memory of having held his hand or rested in his embrace, and the gesture we both made was uncertain. But a beginning. And so we stood, seeing one another for the first time. Beyond the windows the sky was lightening with the pearl-grey of dawn. The birds awoke, and in the corner of the yard, the old rooster, hoarse and imperious, insisted that a new day had begun. Exhaustion overcame us both in that moment. 'It is surely time to sleep now,' he said. 'You have travelled far, and I have talked too much for you. Rest now, and later we can talk again.' I stumbled to the bed in my old corner of the upper chamber and fell deeply into a sleep that felt as if I too was drowning in the welter of experience that he had shared.

I was awake by the third hour, and left the house quietly, needing to find peace among the olive trees just beyond the courtyard. I lost any sense of time as I listened again to his voice in my mind and thought gently about my mother and my sister.

Towards noon I returned to the house and found him waiting. An unaccustomed embrace, that was not unwelcome. I sat beside him on the bench by the gate and shared the bread and raisins, wine and water that the servant brought. He had one more prophetic word to speak, he told me. A true word. Not like any word that he had carried before. This was not made of stone. He had not hewed it from rocks of condemnation found on the high mountains or in the wilderness of judgement. It was a word of hope, a whisper overheard among the olive trees and following the oxen's heavy gait, behind the plough. It had grown in his mind gently, compellingly, and he knew now that it was time to go to the court in Samaria and tell it to the King. 'I am to tell him that God has seen the suffering of the people. Great and small, slave and free, all are suffering, living their lives in fear. There is no one to help them. And the promise of God is true: he will not allow the name of Israel to be blotted out. So he will save them. By the hand of Jeroboam, King of Israel, they will be rescued from fear and their boundaries made secure, so that they may live in peace.'

A word of mercy.

I do not remember much of that day spent in his company. We did not need to speak often. He gave me news of my sister and the hopes of her baby, due in the autumn. I told him something of my life since I left home. He began to prepare for his journey south to the court. He knew, when he returned, that he would be at peace, to remain at the farm for as long as God granted him life. He said, but it was a statement that made no demands for an answer: 'If you choose, your home is here, and the farm is yours.' I did not know then what to reply: a life cannot change direction within the span of a day. He left the words comfortably with me.

Later, we sat at ease together watching the sun drift in clouds of rose and purple into the west, towards the far horizon of the Great Sea. The doves drew near, murmuring and weaving around our feet. We watched them chasing the grain and there was shared contentment for a while.

'I remember your mother so well,' he said, and now there was sadness in his voice and eyes. 'She would take a handful of corn and call to them. They would swoop from the roof to feed from her hand. They let her hold them close for a moment, and then she would let them go free and their wings would flash in the sunlight.' Then he added, regretfully. 'They have not learned to trust me. They come for the corn I scatter, but not to my hand.'

I spoke carefully, words unfamiliar to me, words that I needed him to hear so that he would understand their meaning.

'I think, Father, that if you wait, the doves will learn to trust you. And in time, they will come to your hand.'

No Balm in Gilead

She had been captured as a child by a raiding party and brought there, part play-fellow, part slave, and now utterly lost.

Mistressless. Orphaned. Outcast.

I found her wandering on hillsides resinous with rock rose, clinging to the rough bark of trees, numbly fumbling her way as though blind through the thickets. Cast out, a maid without a mistress. I think he could not bear to look at her, to see her weeping. To remember. A pitiful bundle of clothes wrapped in a shawl was in her hand, and her feet were already bloodied from the rocks and twigs of the goat paths she had followed from the homestead. She gasped as I stepped forward, terror and despair flooding her face as I reached for her hand, pulled her towards me. I soothed her wordlessly, holding her until her trembling had been absorbed into myself, and then taking her with me to my own home. I feared that my father might curse her for a foreigner, but he did not, and my mother took her away to give her water and food to revive her, and to wash and tend her tortured feet. It was as if a great calm held our household, a gentleness, a sorrow. Nothing cruel or violent could be spoken or done, and yet my father, in his prime, had been a great soldier. It was as if the events of these past weeks had turned him away from war, as they had me also, although we had never spoken of it. We took the girl in, and in the months that followed, she and I found in sorrow a way of love together and my parents blessed our marriage.

She told me slowly, as trust grew between us, of the two months they had spent on those hillsides, her mistress Miriam and her friends, camping out in tents of goatskin, gathering the wild gladioli and anemones and making wreaths that no bride would wear. The maidservants began by fetching the water and preparing food, but were drawn into the closeness of their shared life, young women mourning together, for all the childless wombs, the unloved Leahs, the empty breasts, the women never embraced. They grieved for the fast-running, fordless stream between men's vows of war and death and women's instinct for life. It felt, she said, as though it were beyond time, a desolation that they could only lament without understanding its dimensions. Gathering flowers, sharing simple food, telling the stories of their hopes and dreams and fears by day. At night she would lie close to her mistress, huddling together in the kindness of each others' arms, awake, as though staring with rigid eyes at the far stars would delay the dawn. And each morning, the tall pines pointed to the sun's progress through the sky. And each evening their long shadows led back down the valley to her home.

I remember the call to join him. Not as one of his trusted band, the outlaws of Tob who had come with him for the sheer love of fighting and plunder, but one of the hundreds who rallied to him in his campaign against the Ammonites. Here was a leader plucked out of self-banishment, a man who had lived on the outskirts of his tribe fighting in skirmishes against the enemies of Israel for years, and winning a reputation as a ruthless, skilled warrior. Yet never accepted. Son of a prostitute, rejected and despised by his brothers, he carved out a name and legacy for himself in defiance of their contempt. I was with the delegation that sought him out, holding their mules and waiting, as we all were, for the chance to glimpse this man who was already half-legend among us. In our culture it is a shame for the older to beg from the younger, but these old men did so. 'We beg you,' they said. 'Forget the differences of the past. Come and lead us against our common enemy. And you will be the chief of all who live in Gilead.'

Later we heard how he first rejected them, raging with the anger that had scarred and burned him ever since childhood. 'You drove me out, you and all the members of my father's household. Now you come to me to save you. Why do you come to me now?'

They repeated their promise: 'You will be the head of all who live in Gilead. As God is our witness.'

Now I am older, and my own children born and all my heart's longing is for their peace and their inheritance, I can sense his hunger. A man without tribe, without land, without posterity, now promised all that he had desired. A kind of retribution. Their need of his leadership raised him above his half-brothers, gave him the legitimacy of conquest. But he knew nothing of the love of family that leads a man to sow peace for his children. I do not think he had stayed long with his wife and child in the camps he made in the desert of Tob. Constantly moving, leading his band of brigands against the camel trains, against the war bands of the Ammonite Kings, and always gaining a reputation for success; skilled in the war of movement and surprise that such a landscape of hills and desert rocks demands.

I try to understand him, a man who won the reputation of the most feared leader of his generation and yet left no inheritance behind him except his name. There are those who say that he was tender to her, and perhaps to the wife he lost at her birth. One of his companions described her to me, long afterwards. Labouring to please him when he returned weary to the camp at nightfall. Learning from infancy to delight him with the grasp of her tiny fingers around his thumb, and the tilt of her face, listening and listening to the soldiers' tales, though forgotten in a corner. Tales of raid and counter-raid, strategies for holding the hill country and fortifying the towns to secure the territory. She grew to absorb from him his passion for the land, for the story of the journey out of Egypt and the conquest. He spoke out the sagas of the people, and the great battle cry that infused his being: 'What the Lord our God has given us, we will possess.' Dispossessed, birthed in contempt, he had taken to himself a greater cause than local kinship, a call to defend a nation, to mark his name in the records of a nation's history. But in doing so, he became a man of utter ruthlessness. Faithful to his word, implacable, serving an implacable God, dealing always in vows and bargains, dedication and payment. 'The Lord, the Judge,' he proclaimed. He was a weapon in the hand of God, perhaps, and there are those who say that the spirit of God fell on him like a raging fire when he went out against the enemies of Israel. However it was, he set out that day with the stern vow of sacrifice on his lips, bargain for bargain; 'Give me the victory, and I will sacrifice whatever comes first to greet me from my home.'

And it was his daughter, Miriam, dancing like her namesake, with tambourines of celebration.

I can only guess his agony of soul. And marvel at her steadfastness. I like to believe that she did not see the knife's flash at the end, but saw only in his eyes the love and pride he had for her, and the grief.

Among the households of Gilead there was mourning and a sense of dread for what he had done. A nameless uncertainty that such a vow should be fulfilled. No-one dared speak with him, and he took no counsel. A man of inexorable laws. A God whom he believed to be as exacting and as unconditional as himself. A man of no acknowledged birth, who left no child to bear his name or blood to future generations.

In the ensuing months he fought against his own people, Gilead against Ephraim, and the story tells of his contemptuous dealings with them at the fords of Jordan. Forty-two thousand men dying. Perhaps in his exacting mind, there was some terrible bargain outworked there.

Within six years he was dead.

His daughter's death and the slow discovery of my love for her maidservant had ended my young man's dreams of soldiering. I was not there at the fords of Jordan, nor could I sleep for the thought of it, blood flowing endlessly in the river as the slaughter continued. I struggled to find again the faith of our people, to wrestle with the Law that taught us to fulfill our vows, to meet the endless demands of righteousness and sacrifice. To serve an implacable God as he had done? We would lie clenched together, my wife and I, on the heap of goatskins that served us for a bed, each aware of the other, as though the pain connecting us was a bowstring taut between us, talking endlessly through the dark hours until the grey and pale light of early dawn released us to sleep a little before daybreak. We worked to build a stone house, to set walls around it, to herd the goats and tend the olive trees, and she took slow joy in the discovering and planting of herbs and the flowering of apple and pomegranate trees. It seemed, as the spring came, that we also found peace together, full of the hopes of new growth just as the blades of young barley broke through the earth. I had relinquished all thought of spear and sword for the skills of ploughing, and pruning the young vines; we watched the fields we had won from stones and weed turn from green to gold as the crop ripened, and the tender leaves of the vine spread and then came the clustering of our first small bunches of grapes. But as the year passed, with all its promise, there was no sign of a child.

'It is enough,' I told her. 'First we make a home, and then the child will come.' And then, seeing the fear in her eyes. 'I will not stop loving you.'

The years and seasons moved rhythmically, and were marked by festivals and gatherings of the tribe and the nation at the holy places. We went with my parents to Shiloh, and heard the Law recited and brought our sacrifices of thanksgiving and propitiation. At times, travelling Levites would come to our settlement and the families would gather to hear the teaching of the Commandments. And each time, we felt the raw questions we had were unanswered and a fear of even asking them of these men who carried the stern certainty of their God. We would withdraw into the gentleness of the love we found together.

It was seven years before she came to me, to say with hope and joy that at last she dared believe that she carried life. I saw her eyes revive with light that I had learned to live without as she had so often retreated into a quietness that had no peace, only a murmur of the dread of barrenness. Those early months she sang, filled with life as though she were a cup brimming over. Late one afternoon in her fifth month I returned home from the furthermost field where the goats had broken through into the young crop. I was tired as I bent my head and shoulders under the boughs of the old apple tree that we had left for shade more than fruit at the corner of the yard. As I rested my hand on the low lintel of the door and stooped to enter, I realised she was gone. The hearthstone cold, the pitcher empty.

For a little while I stood listening, as though the walls would tell me what must have happened. There was no sign, no overturned pots or trampled rugs. A vacancy where I had learned to expect the warmth of welcome, the promise of food, the gentleness of shared, murmured, loving kindness at the day's end. I searched the yard and nearby fields, already sensing an absence so great that I felt my heart constrict, my throat tighten with calling, and I watched my hands threshing, as though they could scour the air to find her. I could not ask for help in my search, sensing that her need to hide had been so great that even neighbours, kindly as they might be, might violate what little was left of her. Through the night, hearing only the sharp cries of night-walking creatures, and the shifting wind in the hillside trees, I searched further and further in widening circles from our homestead. She could surely not have walked far, encumbered and slowed with child-bearing, but I knew how far panic and dread might have spurred her beyond all reasonable distance.

Slowly I remembered, after many hours, and yet it was all the time the only place. I turned east as the sun rose and climbed the far hillside, brushing the stickiness of resin from my hands as I parted the bushes, calling, calling, as I followed the goats' path to the high ridge and then crossed into pine woods. I found her then, her back braced against a tree's trunk, her hands trailing at her side, and in her lap, a splattering of bright redness, splashing like fresh blood in the spears of the slanting sun. I still cannot speak fully of how it was with us then, as I held her rocking, stiff and cold in my arms, and shuddered at the terror of the night that she had passed. She woke to me, not from sleep, but from some place of withdrawal, like a tomb. Her hands stirred and sifted the glazed brightness of the petals in her lap and I saw that they were anemones, gathered and pooled in a terrible richness of scarlet. 'We gathered them,' she murmured. 'Day after day, to make garlands for her, for each other.'

I lifted her, and all that dreadful redness fell in a trail behind us as I carried her down the slithering hillside path, through the further and nearer fields and to our home. I struck fire in the hearth, poured water, washed, as my mother had done before, the bruised feet, the torn hands, the weary and swollen face. Later we ate a little, and I saw her recover strength enough to know there was life in her and the baby safe. But she would not speak.

For days I hardly dared leave her, staying always within sight of the house, grateful that the crops were sown and I could tether the goats in a corner of the far field and leave them to graze. One evening, as we shared food and I bent to brighten the fire with logs, she spoke again, as though there had been no interval. 'If it is a girl, will she too fall sacrifice to your God if the crops fail, or the enemy draws near, or if some dreadful vow is taken?'

I had no answer for her.

'I know what happened with my own people,' she said. 'The girls could be offered to the gods if the harvest failed, or sold if the family was without food or in debt. When the raiders came, they took us away to be slaves, to be raped at will and discarded if unwanted. I had thought that your God was different, and your people. But it is not so. I have heard them call him the Rock—hard and feelingless!' Her voice jarred, twisted with tears and helpless anger. 'If it is a girl, how will I know that she will be safe? That she will not grow up to be used and thrown aside in the wars, or broken by the vows of your people?'

I turned away from my tears' dazzle of the fire and reached to her, but she flinched away, suddenly rigid, stiffening as I sought to hold her. 'But I promise you,' I stumbled, too swiftly for my thoughts to have formed, and she turned away from me.

'There is no promise you can make to me. I would have sworn that she was the apple of his eye. She believed him as though he were the voice of God himself, and went to her death torn with her grief and dread. She believed it was a solemn vow made to God. There was no escape from it.' Her voice gathered strength, even though shaken by sobs of rage and despair. The days and nights of their vigil on the hillside were more real to her now than all the years of healing and tenderness between us. 'I hear your teachers of the Law. A vow cannot be broken. Every festival a festival of sacrifice. Your enemies slaughtered and their towns put to fire and sword. An unapproachable, dreadful God behind forbidden curtains in a tent. How can I trust you, or the God of your people?'

In the tempest of her distress and helpless anger I feared for the baby even more than I feared for our future together. And I saw that if I spoke or moved clumsily, I might lose her utterly. I held my hands still, open, watching her to see when the storm might collapse within her, when I might gather her in and begin to find some way together.

Slowly, slowly, finding words of gentleness that I drew from some unknown well within me, I brought her back to the place where she knew me, remembered our lives together and the love that had grown to heal us. 'There is only truth,' I said. 'If what you say is true, then we must leave this people and find a way together where we can be free to raise our children. I do not know where, but I swear that I will search with you to find it. But if the truth lies in the God of our people, the God of our Fathers, then we must search for that first.' I felt her withdraw into a place of stillness as I held her, but she did not resist me as I packed the food and filled the skins for a journey and made ready the clothes and rugs that we would need. In the morning, I brought the donkey into the yard, restive at first as I put the rugs and rope on him, and lifted her onto his back. Then we set out to walk to Shiloh.

A four day journey, pausing often to give her chance to ease her back, and for us to take water and simple food of pressed figs, flat bread, raisins. We found hospitality in villages, used to the pilgrim traffic at the festivals and sensing perhaps that our journey was for us a search for the holy place in time of need. The women showed kindness to her, clicking their tongues in wordless rebuke to a husband who would bring her on a journey at such a time, and she allowed them to tend her, her eyes fixed on me as they led her away, but whether with trust or despair, I did not know.

And so we came to the encampment of the Ark. The township had grown around it and it was easy to find lodgings though the price was high, and the place none too clean. The town pulsed to the rhythm of the ceremonies of sacrifice, the lighting of lamps, the ordered rituals. Young men gathered, chanting the words of the Law, and the history of the nation, debating, declaring, preparing themselves under a Master for their work in the villages of the Tribes. Sheep and goats, fattened for sacrifice, doves in baskets, were traded in the streets alongside the clothes and skins, the bread and flour and provisions of every family's life. As I led her through the turmoil of it all I felt her stiffness, the shiver as she passed the tethered goats, the dread reaching me through the touch of her fingertips on my sleeve.

We waited outside the huge tent, I believing that I would know by some instinct of love and yearning, whom to ask. The sun reared itself in the sky, the heat of it pinning us down as my eyes scanned and searched, not even knowing what it was or who it was that I was seeking. Then I saw him. A shrunken old man, brought to a seat by a boy, a grandson perhaps, to sit in the shade near to the entrance of the tent. His head turned towards us and I saw the white glaze of his blind eyes, and felt the deep stillness of his presence. His hearing, acute perhaps, caught the scuff of our feet as I brought my wife to him.

'Sir,' I said, 'I have come to you with my wife.'

Perhaps his blindness gave him senses more acute than sight. He reached out hands to us, drawing us to him, holding our hands and then touching our faces. I watched him take my wife's hand gently but strongly, and then feel the line of her cheek and brow, the silk of her tears wet under his fingers as he stroked back her hair as gently as a mother. 'Come my daughter,' he said. 'You are tired and afraid. Come and sit beside me. Tell me.'

And so I told him. The fear of his rejection, that he would embody the judgement of his God, fled away. He heard patiently, stirring only once when I described the slaughter of Miriam. His silence was itself healing, as though our trouble was held safely at last.

'Long before even the great Moses,' he said, as though to himself, 'Abraham.' He sat very still as though memory was stirring in him, and beyond and before memory, ancestral journeys of our people from times unknown. 'It was to Abraham that God revealed himself in ancient times,' he said. I watched him swaying gently with the rhythm of his words, not like the frenzied rocking and chanting of the teachers of the Law that we had passed, but like a man who flows effortlessly with the stream of his story. 'Our forefather Abraham walked with God as a friend, a man whose story is full of questions and failure, years of uncertainty and waiting. It was to Abraham that the preciousness of life was revealed. He took his son to the point of sacrifice and learned that it was not the will of God to take human life as an offering. He followed the way of obedience, but he was shown that this sacrifice was not what was asked of him. Nor is it asked of us.'

In the stillness that followed his words, I felt my wife trembling.

'I regret,' he said. 'I will regret always that I did not reach the man Jephthah before he took her life away. Perhaps if I or one of my fellow priests had spoken with him he might have understood that his vow was not required of him—a vow that defies every commandment not to kill, not to follow the ways of the Canaanite tribes who sacrifice their sons and daughters to win the favour of their gods!' His voice had risen, shaking with both grief and anger. 'In the unrest of those days, I did not hear until long after the day of her death. Blind and old as I was even then, I would have gone, and told him that the God he thought would bind him to such a vow was the same God who would willingly release him. It was a vow taken in hardness of heart, a vow that assumed that God is to be bargained with, who deals like a trader in the marketplace. A man whose life was shaped by rejection and harshness.' He sat still, veined hands still shaking with his distress.

'So, my daughter,' he said, very gently. 'You need not fear the God of your husband's people. The stories tell us of Abraham, who was not afraid to argue with God. They tell us too about his wife, Sarah, whom God called a Princess, and she was not afraid to laugh in the presence of God. That laughter became the name of her son, and she is the mother of us all. Her confidence in God is remembered always. That is the truth that you need to know and live with.'

He stirred and beckoned towards his grandson who sat on his haunches some yards away from us. 'Bring us bread and wine, and water to refresh these friends after their travels,' he said smiling at the boy. Then, 'Do you know what lies within this great Tent?' he asked. He must have sensed my wondering slow shake of the head, for I had lost words and my wife was silent. 'It is a great mystery, and it holds us in worship, but we sometimes forget,' he murmured, as though half to himself. 'At the very heart of the Tent, in the place where only the High Priest can enter, is the Ark of the Covenant. But the true name of that Ark is the mercy seat, the place not of judgement but of mercy. The deepest, closest place to God is the place of his mercy, not his Law. We are already forgetting that even as we teach the rules and regulations of the Law to the tribes.'

In the coolness of the evening we sat with him and he spoke of many things, describing all that he understood of the history of the people and of the kindness of the God he had come to know best in old age. He took us to his home, and his shrivelled wife welcomed us with bright eyes set deeply in crevices of laughter and kindness. They gave us shelter and shared their food, and in the morning, blessed us for the journey and for the birth. And so we set out, still silent, except for our thanks, but healed in heart and at one with one another.

We came home. A cold hearth, a still house, but no longer a place of dread. For nearly four months we waited with growing hope, until one evening I sent word to my mother and the village women to come to tend her while I walked the boundaries of the farm, and prayed and struggled with my fears and hopes as she struggled to bring life into the world. In the grey hours of dawn, as faint stars gave way to the gathering light of the sun, I heard the cry. A thin bleat of life, and then my mother calling, 'Eliab, Eliab! Come, come quickly!' Then as I ran, 'Zepha has a baby! Come quickly!' So I ducked under the lintel, and pushed through the women tenderly, excitedly gathered around her.

'Look, Eliab,' my wife said, exhausted, proud. 'You have a daughter.'

I took her in my arms, a great breath of joy breaking out of my heart. 'Our daughter,' I said, 'Zepha, our daughter!'

I looked from daughter to wife, and spoke what we had agreed as we had travelled together all those months ago as we returned from Shiloh. 'Her name is Sarah,' I said. 'She will be a woman of laughter. And fear will never come near her.'

Speaking in Riddles

To my Dear Son, Jacob.

Greetings to you, to your wife and to your sons, my grandsons, whom I long to see.

I beg you, after these long years of separation, to read this letter and understand something of the events that drove us apart. Since then, we have never spoken: I yearn for us to be reconciled. I sense that little time is left to me.

Few fathers can have had the joy that I felt all those years ago, when I saw you, my son, rise up to address the Council of elders and gain their respect. That respect was not given to you for your father's sake, but because of your own devotion to the Law and tradition of our people; your earnest quest for righteousness. From childhood, you had been my pride and the deepest satisfaction of my ambitions—I believed that you were my legacy for our people and community, a legacy that would last long after my death. Perhaps that is why the gulf between us is now so wide.

You will, I think, remember that day, more than twelve years ago now, when I was sent from the Council to question the Galilean. The stories that had gathered around him of miracles of healing and deliverance were disturbing rumours that could unsettle the careful balance of our way of life. How precarious our lives were, even then. When you are a child, you play the game of keeping to the squares in the paving, avoiding the cracks as you jump from one to another. We saw ourselves as the guardians of our nation, our traditions, and so we kept all safe by walking delicately, ever more carefully avoiding the cracks between the stones. Until that day. That morning a storm had blown into the Temple courts, a great wind that blew to overturn the counting tables, sending animals stampeding into the streets and the doves flying from their wicker baskets. A storm of passion, an authentic prophetic voice unheard for centuries: *You have turned my Father's house into a marketplace!*

The wind, he said to me that evening, *will blow as it chooses.* That day it blew away the compromises that had gathered around our Temple worship and overturned all our careful structures of survival. When he was challenged about his authority to do such a thing, he answered only in riddles: *I will show you a temple that can be destroyed and rebuilt in three days.*

There was, of course, a hurriedly convened Council meeting and then the decision to send me to talk with him. I was chosen simply because I was the oldest member present, the one most likely to remind him of the respect due to the rulers of his people. Old enough, I realised, to have seen a glittering temple built, a country brutally conquered, passionate convictions wax and wane with time. Even prophets, aspiring messiahs and freedom fighters: I had watched them come and go, and we had kept our careful balance under occupation.

But as I walked from the meeting, I found that I had taken his words with me. *My Father's house.* I felt them turning and turning restlessly in my mind and memory until I recognised him. A Passover feast nearly twenty years ago. A boy on the threshold of manhood, listening carefully to those of us who were explaining the Law and the prophecies regarding the future of Israel. A boy of much the same age as you were at that time, my son, all those years ago, questioning us closely and drawing on the Scriptures from the wisdom of Job and prophecies of Isaiah to stir us to new and disturbing insights. Then there was a bustle and his family entered, reproaching him. He answered his mother very firmly, though very courteously: *You did not need to search for me. You knew I had to be in my Father's house.* Hearing him again, I knew, as I walked to where he was staying that night, that this was no hothead from the north with enticing visions and words of revolt, no shooting star in the desert sky. A man of learning, rooted in the Scriptures, a man who spoke of the Temple in a way that was unique, and of God (whose very name we may not utter), with grave familiarity as *Father*.

He was staying with John bar Zebedee's family, who had a house in Jerusalem in those days, and they had set aside for him a small room at the top of the house. I found him there, waiting quietly, looking out over the rooftops towards the mountains. There was a cluster of oil lamps and a welcoming brazier of coals. It was dark and chill: the spring warmth had not touched the evening air. Night can be a good time for talking: there is quiet and freedom from interruption. Leaning towards the fire, and offering wine and dates, he waited for my prepared statement: a courteous acknowledgement of his teaching and the miracles that had been reported to us, and of his clear devotion to God. The words hung between us: true, polite, inadequate. The coals flared, I remember, and a gust of wind stirred the lamp flames. He laughed, and spread his hands in a generous gesture that I learned was characteristic. In his eyes there was a spark of energy, a passion for argument that reminded me my student days. *You want to talk about the origin of things? I tell you that you won't be able to identify anything of the Kingdom of God unless you have been reborn.*

Reborn! I'm an old man! How can I re-enter the womb of my mother and begin life again? We both strode into the argument, enjoying the challenge, word against word, meaning against meaning. But even as I spoke, I thought about birth and death, about the careful patterns of my life and certainties of my faith, all at stake in this hour, this moment. Small sounds and movements, the splutter of a lamp's wick, the call of a man in the street outside, filled the gap between the words where I sensed the end of one life and the beginning of another. How can I explain to you, Jacob, what this meant to me? I wrestled with the words as I had wrestled as a young man in the village, instep against instep, to resist this man whose gentle laughter threatened to overthrow me and all my years of scholarship. I have seen birth: the struggling grasp of freedom in the cries and clenching fingers of the new born before our women bind them with linen clothes to straighten and still their bodies. My answer showed how close I knew myself to be to that other birth, death itself, with its grave bandages that hold the body in an ordered peace before the great mystery of life beyond the tomb.

How can an old man like myself re-enter his mother's womb and be re-born? I challenged him, knowing full well the matching of riddle for riddle was sustained whilst underneath the words, the structures of Law and tradition, the careful, visible systems and regulations by which we worship God, fell, crashed, surrendered. Everything that I had upheld for the survival of our nation. *The origin of all human systems is human: mortal, fallible, earth-bound,* he answered. *But the origin of spiritual things and the Kingdom of God itself must be spiritual. So don't be surprised when I say to you that you, and all of Israel, require a new and spiritual birth. A birth conceived by the Spirit of God, who blows wherever he wants: unpredictable, invisible, uncontrollable. The old systems and regulations are over. Everything we are showing you is a sign of the invisible Kingdom. Only the Son of Man knows and reveals these things because his origin is heaven.* He smiled again, patiently, gently, as I struggled to resist, to argue, to grasp his meaning even as it demolished my own. *You are a teacher of the people,* he said, shrugging expressively, *and you don't understand! But I want to lead you to the things of heaven.* Then he took as his example one of the most perplexing acts of Moses in the Books of the Law, giving again a riddle for me to solve: Moses and the serpent. *Like that,* he said. *The Son of Man will be lifted up before the people, so that all who believe in him will have eternal life.*

Then he took me beyond Moses and the traditions of our nation to the purposes of God long before the Law given on Sinai. Purposes set in motion on the earth in the promises given to Abraham, brought to fruition now, and shared with me despite all my hesitation and resistance. The whole world loved by God. Israel destined as a blessing for all the nations. The only Son of God sent from heaven itself to bring the certainty of eternal life to all who believe in him. Not condemnation for those outside the Law, but the whole world reconciled to God.

I know my dear Son that you have clung with integrity to the traditions of the Law and its path of righteousness all your life. I know that you could not understand or forgive the path that I took—and I took it hesitantly at first, but then with growing certainty. I watched with sorrow and then with horror the traps that were set for him by men I had considered friends, who now spied constantly on his movements and reported his words to the Council. You remember the crisis for me, more than a year after that first meeting, when I challenged the Council again, using the Law itself as my grounds for appeal. It was on that day that they turned me out of the meeting with contempt. I do not know how you felt: I tried to meet your eyes across the Council chamber but saw only your anger. You felt that I brought shame on you and your family that day. Forgive me for wounding you, Jacob. If the Law meant anything to me, and it had been the lamp to my path all my life, it was expressed in the words of Micah: to act justly, to love mercy, to walk humbly before God. And so I made my choice.

A year later it was finished. And begun.

Perhaps you knew that I went with Joseph to the tomb after that mockery of a trial and the brutal execution. We wrapped his body in the winding clothes of death and with spices to honour a king. I know, and I saw with my own eyes, that he was raised from death, born again out of the constriction of the tomb, speaking peace and forgiveness, not judgement or vengeance, before returning to heaven, his origin, his Father's house.

And now my Son, I live gratefully with Joseph and his family, but my eyes often turn south-east towards the hills of Jerusalem as I think of you. I have grown fearful of what may be your future. I sense a tide of devastation coming towards the city: proud buildings overthrown, stone by stone, a weeping widowhood, and our people scattered. Let me have news of you. I am old now, and wait in this corner room, trusting that you will receive this letter, watching and praying for your safety and that your heart will turn to me. I have put together the fragments of my memories so that you may understand, and that you also might ponder the riddles and mysteries of truth. So I ask you: *How can an old man be re-born and an ancient nation revived? What does a serpent on a pole in the desert have in common with a man who died on a pole of crucifixion? What kind of temple can be demolished and rebuilt in three days?* Always you have pursued the truth. Supposing the truth is not found in the struggle to keep to perfection the commandments of the Law but in conversation with a man who claimed to be the Son of God and said that above all else, God loved the world?

Remember also the riddle of your own name: *A wrestler wins by being overthrown; a prince victorious only in defeat.*

Peace to you, and to your family, Jacob, my beloved son.

I long to see your face.

Nicodemus

That Night

Silent feet, silent tongue. That is how they train you. And we don't tell them: sharpened ears, sharpened sight. We see and hear everything. When we can snatch the odd time off, between dinner and bed, maybe, or in the heat of the afternoon when the mistress is resting, we meet up in the market place, or the wine shops down the alley by the Gate, and catch up on the gossip. We all know one another, share the same secret life. Comradeship. Where the mask can slip a little. Small jokes. Kindness. Maybe even the hope of a future husband or a wife, if the small savings can be garnered away and the luck turns. Who knows?

But this evening. How can I begin to talk of it? It's very late now, but there are still lights in many houses, and torches carried along the streets, and the crunch of soldiers' feet, the scuff and scurry of sandals, and a distant murmur of unrest, like the growl in the back of a wild dog's throat. The wild dogs that hang around the rubbish, snarling.

Sharpened ears, sharpened sight.

I'm trying to sort it in my head. Who I was, even yesterday, is not who I feel I am today. It began, I think, with that odd moment by the well. I'd drawn up the water, filled the great jar, and was hoisting it up to carry it through the streets, the last of many, but this one to be carried upstairs to the guest room.

I was tired. Maybe I've always been tired, since the day my father sold me in payment of his debts. Just out of childhood, twelve years old, and I remember my mother weeping. Down in the dust, begging him. And he shook her off, and sent me north to the city with a friend of his, in a cart full of new wineskins, and goatskin rugs, stinking and hot, and I sat still as stone and the tears have never come. You could say I was lucky. When I hear other stories, I know that's true in a way. I came to the house of a good woman and her family, none of them cruel or rough, and she put me in the care of the steward and the cook to train me to serve at table, and to learn to prepare the food. They were kind, mostly, except when the household got very busy at the festivals, and once a year I was given a gift of money, and clothing, and the hope grew that one day, they might set me free. Although, when you think about it, freedom is a blade with two edges, and one points towards you. There's no life in those dark and churning streets for a woman on her own. Ten years since I came, just a child, and now I carry the water and attend to guests, and serve at table, silent, watchful. Just a pair of hands, really, until those odd hours of fleeting laughter and talk in the stolen moments of the day or night.

So, I'd filled the great pitcher, and turned, feeling the balance of it, straightening up to begin the walk to the house, and a man stopped me. 'Daughter,' he said. 'Let me carry that for you.' I thought he was joking, or if not, maybe it was one of the slaves like myself, wanting to give me a hand. But men don't carry the water. That's a woman's job.

'No,' I said, slowly facing him, unsure how to deal with this. If it was a joke, it was a bad one. If it was a genuine offer of help, I needed to be sure that I could trust this man, and know he was not looking for any favours. I looked: I had never seen him before, and even though I looked hard at him, I could not tell you the details of his face.

'My daughter,' he said again. 'You are very tired. Let me take this for you.' As I looked at him, I felt as if he knew me, and I was afraid that the crying might begin and never stop. 'Don't worry,' he said, very gently, and took the heavy jar, and balanced it carefully, and walked away. A few heads turned as he walked up the street, and a couple of men began to follow him. Gathering myself as soon as I could, I followed too, anxious and hot as the sun was now moving further overhead. But I need not have worried. He took the pitcher to the house, climbed the outside steps to the upper room, while the two men behind him went inside to talk to the master. They had taken no notice of the man. As I came near to the door, he came downstairs, smiled, and was gone. I went to the back of the house, puzzled, silent. Then the master of the house came in almost immediately and gave directions for the upper room to be prepared for thirteen guests to eat the Passover meal.

There was then no time to waste. Food to prepare, not just for the family, but for these guests. The room to be spotless and the furniture and cushions ready for them to recline around the long table. Lamps to be set out and wicks trimmed. The pitcher of water, the jug, bowl and towels for their feet to be washed. My job, before the meal could be served. You could tell, from the whispered excitement in the house, that these were important guests, and everything must be perfect. The silent, sharp-eyed service that I was trained for.

The sun turned red and sank lazily beneath the clouds that rise from the Great Sea, far west—and I have never seen it, but so they tell me. Dusk gathered in corners, and spread slowly over the city and the lamps were lighted, and torches flared in the streets. I remember standing at the doorway, out of sight, as the men came up the stairs, bringing with them the sweat and restlessness of the day and its dust in their hair and clothing, and on their feet and sandals. I stood ready with the bowl and jug and towels, waiting for them to take their ease on the cushions around the low table. They were excited, talking and gesturing as they took their places and I noticed, as you do, the way in which they pushed for position to lie near the head of the table.

They did not notice as I moved forward, expecting to kneel and begin the task of easing their feet and cleansing them for the meal ahead. Nor did they notice as he came in, and as he silently took the bowl and jug and towel from me, and began my work, the slave's work. Finger on lips to me, and that same steady look, the gentle smile, then the intense focus on the feet of his friends, washing them with great tenderness, as if caressing them with kindness. At first they thought it was the slave: so familiar was the pattern of hospitality, they barely recognised that it was happening. Then one of them, a burly man who seemed, by the strength of his voice and presence to have some sort of leadership, swung round and realised. He was loud in his protests, loud with the strong accent of the north, but his friend, who I see now was the true leader of the group, persisted. I saw his red-faced embarrassment as he submitted, and the rest of the group, frozen, I thought, speechless, as their leader washed their feet and dried them, carefully. Tenderly. It takes a long time to wash twelve pairs of feet. The room waited, the meal forgotten, and the evening gathered itself around the table. I felt the darkness waiting as if about to spring. The oil lamps held it at bay.

Then at last the figures came to life. The meal began and I ran to and fro with the platters of meat and bread, the wineskins to pour into the jugs and then to cups—and it takes a steady hand—and all the special ceremonial food of the Passover. I watched them, and listened as the conversation rose, with argument and flourishes of hands and arms and food and cups spilt onto the table. 'Who's the most important?' They were saying. 'Which of us will be in the place of power when the kingdom comes?'

'Well,' I thought to myself. 'Have you learned nothing?' But I had to go then and get more food and more to drink. When I returned, the group had quietened. 'Is it me, is it me?' They were saying, but I do not know the question.

There was one moment as I lingered when he stood and took the break and broke it, tore it apart, and said a strange thing. 'My body,' he said and handed it to them.

When I went back, to clear the table, one of them was rising to his feet, and leaving hurriedly, and the stir of air at his passing caused all the lamps to splutter and the darkness entered as he left. I brought light quickly and renewed the lamps but the mood had changed. They shifted uncomfortably, then stood together to sing the psalm and left down the steps and into the dark streets.

I did not get away until much later that night, after the first cockcrow, but you could sense that rising murmur of excitement, anger, fear, call it what you like, it was all those things, and the city still hums with it. I joined old friends at the wine shop and heard the stories that were running round like jackals. Malchus, slave of the high priest, came with the news of arrest and betrayal in the garden, clutching his ear and we all marvelled at his story, and touched his ear, and the tale grew of the man in the garden and the followers who ran away. Anna came bursting in with the excitement of her story, always a gossip. 'I recognised him, I tell you,' she said, hands on hips. 'He was one of them, one of those men from Galilee. You could tell it by his voice. And I've seen him around with that Jesus. Big fellow, but not so big now, I can tell you. Three times he said he didn't know him.' Others came with the details of the show trial at the high priest's and then Herod, and we knew the next step would be the Romans. The taste of the story turned bitter to all of us and we found ourselves scattering, even the most talkative frightened by the events that were overtaking us, events of great heaviness, terrible things. I thought of the man. He had called me, 'Daughter'. No-one had done that since the day I left my home, a slave.

Two of my friends were walking up ahead as I returned through the alleys to the house. Fragments of their talk reached me, and stay with me now. 'They say he sold him for thirty pieces of silver,' they were saying.

The slave price. The price my father got for me.

Through a Glass, Darkly

Your present is always my past. Your perceptions of what and who I am are like drifts of cloud, through which I move freely. I feel the sting, the astringency of your judgements, but you cannot shame me again. There is too much laughter, too much eager anticipation here for that. But in diminishing me to fit the size of your interpretation you also diminish him, making him speak with your voice and not daring to hear the outrageousness of his words or see his uninhibited gestures and expression.

We laugh here when we glimpse how we are spoken of and written about. It is an aching laughter sometimes, as it was when we saw how the leaps we took forward into freedom became locked and chained in immobility within two generations. We say here that a day is like a thousand years and a thousand years as one day: we live in time vertically, not only horizontally, exploring depth and height as well as length and breadth of experience. Sometimes we feel the passing of time and know its painful slowness, watching history with you as a parent watches a fevered child's sleep. At other times we live in an intensity of knowing: detailed, vivid, unforgettable. That day for me was as a thousand years. The seconds, moments, words, expressions live in my memory as the rings of a tree show its life.

But I am talking too much, as I always do. Always I loved to talk, to argue. I wanted to know, to explore, to escape. Here, as on that day, I found at last that all questions can be answered and conversation has no limits of time or misunderstanding. You already know my story, but not its fullness, not its reality. You have time's pane of glass to look through: hand-blown, flawed, distorting. But come with me: see and hear afresh.

There is the village. Shapes waver in the heat. A group is coming over the brow of the hill: they separate and one comes on alone, his shadow shrunk beneath the soles of his feet. And there am I, walking, I remember, with that strange mixture of defiance and caution, stepping close to the buildings, hand balancing the jar against my hip, chin tilted, eyes sidelong. That is how I walked then. The street seemed long and empty and each day, whispers ran along it, stirring up the dust around me.

A man, a woman. Converging. He sits on the low wall of the well, waiting. I recognise even from a distance that he is a Jew. I know my position: woman, divorcee, inferior race. Watch him closely. He should draw back so that even his clothes cannot be brushed by me, his eyes should be averted. If he speaks at all, it should remind me of my subservience. But he looks up, looks directly at me and I become still, the water jar empty in my hands. There is a huge moment of quietness between us and the day's heat presses down on us both. It is his need, not mine that bridges the gap, and I am amazed that he should put himself in debt to me. I blurt out questions as I pull on the rope that raises the wooden bucket to the surface, and pour water into the pitcher and then into his cupped hands. He should ignore me, for what man even of my own race would enter into discussion with a woman?

Instead, he answers, after raising the water long and gratefully to his mouth, and then pouring it over his head and neck as I replenish his hands. He speaks of a gift, a giver, and then, laughing, receives a fresh outpouring into his cupped palms and throws it up into the air, a spangling of brightness between us: *living water!* But I did not then understand. I saw only the well, holding its old and dark depths of water and the struggle of raising it to the surface to wash and cook and water the flocks. A daily toil, regular, necessary: a place of weary history, connecting a despised-as-bastard people with their heritage.

He saw the weariness. I think he saw all things, but did not tell me until I was ready to trust him. He looked directly at me: passion without lust, authority without dominance. *You are always going to be thirsty, always returning for more. I can give you a spring of water that is alive within you, a spring of water that will never run dry but will flow into eternity.* And I remembered in a flash of vividness a brief moment of my childhood, running behind my cousin as he loped up the hillside to watch the goats. He showed me the hidden spring, breaking out of the stones beneath a rock fall at the edge of the pasture, and I dipped my hands in its coldness and splashed and played. *Living water.* Beyond price, beyond comparison with this ancient pit and the heave of the bucket from its depths.

Suddenly, we returned to time and to the present. I was alone with a stranger, and I was already a woman of no reputation. He sought to cover my vulnerability: *Go quickly, get your husband and return.* I have heard it said that this was a trick to expose and shame me. Not so. It was for me to take the steps that lead to truth. And as I answered, *I have no husband,* he responded out of his knowledge of my life, knowledge that was far beyond the words and facts that you have read and have judged me by. He knew that first and dreadful marriage contracted between a twelve year old girl and an older man and the terror and pain of those days, and the glad relief of widowhood. He knew too the search for love *(you are always going to be thirsty)* in a series of marriages ending in divorce and desperation and the barrenness of those couplings. A childless woman does not age in body like her contemporaries, but her spirit dies, and her name is extinguished. The man I lived with now had given me a hearth and a roof, but not a name to cover me, and I knew it would not be long before I was turned out.

You have spoken the truth. He made it a commendation.

No ordinary man spoke like this, direct, compassionate. I voiced the little I knew of our heritage, our shared ancestral religion and the wound of separation that lay between us. *You are a prophet.* Then my questions bubbled up, sensing a permission I had never had, a permission to ask questions thought beyond the understanding of a woman. *Why, when we worship on the mountain of blessing here according to Moses and the elders, why do you Jews say that the only place of true worship is Jerusalem?* You can hear the frustration, the ache of rejection: a despised people and a despised woman who had no place even in her own community. The truth of my own selfhood was naked there, and if there had been no answer, there was nowhere I could have gone from this encounter.

He answered, *Trust me.* And he set worship free from mountains and temple rituals, traditions and divisive histories. *You will worship the Father.* He spoke again and again of truth and true worshippers, including me as he spoke, including all the separated and rejected ones. *The Jews are the channel through which salvation comes, but the Father is searching for all those who will worship him in spirit and in truth. And that worship is free of boundaries and races.* I did not know how to answer him. A half-forgotten legend. The Messiah-deliverer, the hope of his people? I breathed it out, and he spoke again, looking me full in the face, entrusting me with a message, with his identity as I had entrusted him with mine: *I am he. The one speaking to you now.*

Even as we looked at one another, the silence between us, which held more than words, was broken with the scuffle of feet as his friends returned. I sensed their hostility, their suspicion, the secretive withdrawal of their eyes and the scrape of their sandals as they stepped back to make room for me to leave. But no-one spoke. It was in that instant that I returned to the passing of time; the growth of the shadows, the weight of the water jar in my hands. I had lived and drunk deeply of hope.

I left the water jar at the well, and slowly at first, then with quicker and quicker steps ran for the village, calling out as I ran, *Come and see, this man told me everything about myself. Can this be the Messiah?* And they came. You know the story of their coming and the amazed acceptance of this man and the words of hope and love he brought. You know what they said. *We can believe now, not just because of your words, but we have heard for ourselves. He is the Saviour of the world.* You look back on our story with hindsight, and perhaps do not see, as I still see, how huge those leaps of revelation were, made to a woman and to a despised community.

This man told me everything about myself. It was not a litany of shame. I knew that already. Women who live by their wits and their bodies on the edge of their communities already know the details and histories of their immorality and his knowledge of me set me free from that. What he did was to hold all of my being, past and present, and give it identity again. To console what had been broken and abused and to wash the scorching brand of guilt with cool water. To restore the potential for love and relationship. To give me dignity.

So I began to live again, in a community that opened itself to kindness and acceptance, that had glimpsed healing spreading beyond the boundaries of Judea to despised Samaria, and to the world. I found shelter and work within a family that opened its arms to me. When the time seemed right I went with others to visit Jerusalem and was part of that Passover week of triumph and horror and amazement, finding myself among the women who stood when the closest friends fled, and who first heard of the astonishment of the empty tomb and the stumbling words of resurrection. After those days we lived on the brink of miracles, the outpouring of living water that was endless in its supply, flooding from Jerusalem through Judea and Samaria and out into the world. News and excitement reached us constantly on the roads with the passing of merchants and traders. Others came to sit at the well, wearied with their journey, and glad of the cool water offered and the hospitality of the village.

One such was the man I married, yes, in my old age! A man with his own tale of rejection and miracle, a one-time leper healed and grateful, on his way to recover his lost inheritance in a northern village and then go south west to the coast, to Joppa, to begin work again as a potter, with fingers restored from numbness and gifted again with their old skills. As he returned through the village he asked for my hand, and I accepted, glad of the love and kindness of this gentle man, and with the promise of shared stories of healing and thankfulness to warm us. There too in Joppa there were miracles. But you know of them.

My name, you see, and perhaps you can see clearly now, is Dorcas.

Inheritance

I was born in the midst of the long journey.

A new-born cry among the tents and the women chirping and soothing as the baby was washed and scooped to its mother's breast. Later, after the due time, he thrust his wide shoulders, they told me, through the tent opening and demanded me, his wife laughing proudly at his huge hands curving around my smallness. A broad, vigorous old man, giving me his little finger to suck, then lifting me high as he strode out into the desert and held me up to the roof of the sky. A celebration. Dancing, songs of their travelling. And all the time, a dying generation.

I was his last-born after many years and his only daughter. Perhaps he knew he was man enough to delight in a daughter, rather than demand another son from the silent heavens and his compliant but henceforth barren wife. He never made me feel that he regretted that I was a little girl as he taught me to walk and climb among the rocks and gullies of the wilderness. Later, as I grew bold and questioning, he rehearsed the long sagas of the journey, chanting with me the rhythms of the laws and the tales of our fathers as we sat around the fires at night. After dark he would take me beyond the safety of the tents, ignoring the fears and pleas of my mother, and fill my head with awesome tales of the great deliverance, the meaning of the lustrous glowing column that swayed beyond the camp, and describe the waiting land beyond the desert. And I would gaze at him, the moonlight catching his white hair and beard, and he grew taller in my imagination as he pointed out the great constellations so that I thought of him as only a little less than Orion, the great hunter of the skies.

My mother taught me, lovingly, the duties and skills of a wife. Much younger than he, she had never fully known the bondage of old ways, and she would carry water proudly on her head or hip, prepare the food, keep the clothes and bedding clean and comfortable. She honoured him and loved the laughter and the fearlessness that he brought to us as his gift every evening and the deep-rooted hope he carried for the future. *I saw,* he would say, *I know. And it will be.* I learned from him the passion for freedom that has enkindled my whole life. *Never return to slavery,* he said, showing me once the deep-cut scars across his back and shoulders. *They were given me with my name in another life and in another place. I will not speak of it again.* So I grew up, alone, although I did not feel it as loneliness. My brothers had joined the men of the tribe in military training. There were children that I played with. Later, young men kept their distance, sensing my father's standing in the community. Girls that I had known as a child became old enough to marry and bring their babies into this world that we inhabited. A world of tents gathered around oases and springs; the ceaseless rhythms of food and the necessity of water; the sacred festivals and the mighty pronouncements of the Leader; the waves of awe that bowed us down like rushes before the desert wind; the packing up and moving on. And all the time, men younger than he, dying every day, and the women too. Eventually, my mother among them. The wailing of the mourners drifted daily through the camp, a thread of grief that we wove into our lives, weaving it poignantly with the hope that promised us a new beginning for all those born as I was, after the wandering began.

The day came when we turned west and waited at the River, on the edge, as it were, of a new land, the land promised. An army led by its priests and with its rearguard, the women and children. No old men or old women. None except my father and his companion, now our Leader. A young nation, poised for conquest, reclaiming, so the histories told us, the land walked by our forefathers. I felt their presence in the wind lifting our banners, the sun smiting the gold of the sacred ark so that the light split into shards of brilliance. I saw my father, old as he was, amongst the foremost of the captains of the host. Impassioned for the struggle ahead, he carried with him the younger men, stirring them to courage. That day, and for many days, the nation renewed its vows, was reborn in the waters of the River, prepared itself for its inheritance. Then moved forward as one, to begin the struggle.

Those early months and years of campaigning have blurred in my memory. The men returned to the camp, bloodied and weary. Sometimes their triumph was palpable; sometimes ashamed and ashen they returned with tales of losses and defeat. Then the lament of grief and fear would rise from the tents and the nation would huddle together in the valleys of encampment to call out to God for guidance and victory. I do remember clearly the very first days of harvest, when the barley grains poured though our cupped hands and we learned, but as if we had always known, the old skills of winnowing chaff from grain, and the rhythm of circling stone on stone to turn the hard seed into soft flour. That day, the miracles of wafer gathered in the dew of the morning ceased, and the new miracle began, of flour and oil transformed into bread, savoured and shared and eaten at our firesides. I remember also, though I was never in the forefront of the fighting, the tales of terror, of fleeing families whose villages we discovered with the hearth fires still warm, of the screams of women and children caught by the soldiers. I would like to believe that their ending was swift and that there was no prolonging of their terror in rape or torment. Men shrug and say, *It is war.* Now even after all these years, I hear that sound in my mind, and the questions rise up unanswered.

But Jericho stands out in my memory, and for this reason. After the siege and its miraculous ending, the city was devoured by fire and its people, man, woman and child, and all its living creatures, slain. One family was brought out alive, Rahab and her parents, her brothers and sisters and their families. Kept safe, crowding trembling in their house built into the city wall, they were rescued because of a red rope, a sign between her and the spies who had found refuge in her house. For days after the capture of her city she and her family lived in the huddle of their few possessions, outside the camp. They had been salvaged from destruction, but there was no willingness to take them within the shelter of the camp or offer them belongingness. Alone, but carrying my authority as my father's daughter, I sought them out, bringing them within the shelter of my own tent, sharing the bread we had learned to bake, the wine of our first harvest and water from the spring. Gradually they were accepted, and even some years later, marriages took place which drew them fully into the community of the tribe of Judah. Rahab married a man of good family and later went to live in the northern hill country, at Bethlehem, far away from my father's conquered town of Hebron and its territory and the village where I settled after my marriage. But we had become close friends, sisters, and so remained despite all the miles between us. Each year we met on the Day of Remembering, the Festival of Passover, when the Tribes gather.

Rahab's friendship sustained me in those years of campaigning, the years when I, unmarried, kept my father's tent and offered hospitality, mending and preparing his clothes and equipment and packing up camp amidst the fighting. We fetched water, ground flour, gathered wood for the fires together all through the gradual settlement and then the dismemberment of the mighty encampment and the separation of tribe and tribe according to their allotment of land. She taught me her story, a woman's story. A girl child given to the priests of their gods by her parents in the terror of their devotion; a young woman trapped in ritual prostitution; an awakening to her own identity and her careful escape at a time when her city's leaders and priests were preoccupied with the invasion of the land. Her value had declined with maturity, and so it was not difficult to fade away from the processions and dances for the gods, pleading sickness and feigning an aging weariness that released her to return to the house of her parents. There she worked with them to run the inn that they kept, set in the city walls. And it was there that she met and hid the spies from our camp and gained for herself, and her whole family, release from the destruction that overtook the entire city.

When I returned to the family, she told me, and we both wept in the telling, *my father stood apart, afraid that the priests would take some terrible retribution on us. But my mother, in secret, held me and rocked me in her arms, crying again and again with the remembered pain of separation. We found healing together, and strength, and as weeks passed and there was no summons from the priesthood, even my father began to believe that we could live at peace together. I had been rescued from horror, and my joy gave me strength to forgive them and even to understand and pity their fear and weakness. And all around us, a new terror was seizing the people of the city, the dread of your army and of the marching god of your armies who seemed to give you success at every turn. But I had known the worst of fear and shame and for me this invasion could only bring hope—a god, who if I served him, offered greater protection than the rituals and deceptions of my people. And so it was.* Here she smiled gently, and took my hand. There were no more words.

Years later, she turned her story into songs, songs she sang to her babies and to her grandchildren, as they will teach their children's children:

I was in a besieged city,
But the God of rescue showed me love.
Nobody heard my cries for help but him!

Or,

Always wait for God,
Be strong and do not fear,
Wait for his coming.

A great favourite was:

I am a bird that escaped from the net
I am a bird that flies free in the air.

They are the songs that we mothers teach our children to remember the story, to hold people in our minds as the living and not the dead. I have my own, and sing them to my daughter's children. They love to hear, *Caleb said go up!* And the song of my inheritance, the song of my field.

But I run ahead of my story.

My father, as strong and skilled in age as he was in youth, laid claim to the hill country of Hebron as his inheritance, according to the promises of more than forty years before, and drove out the inhabitants and established us, our family, in that neighbourhood. *Caleb the Wholehearted* was his name among the Tribes, before the great separation was completed, and that is how he is remembered. As peace came, and we learned what it was to sow and harvest, to tend the sheep and goats, and build and dwell in houses of stone that did not move with the wind or glimmer with moonlight, so he turned to me with an understanding that all my youth had gone. I was much more than twenty, old I felt, with watching and wandering, but he saw me still as a beloved daughter, and sought a marriage for me. I think he wanted me to have as a husband a man like himself, a man of courage and leadership, and so my husband proved to be, Othniel, my cousin. He brought me all that he knew of love and faithfulness and we had children and happiness in their growing. Like my father, he was strong and vigorous in age, and led the nation as its Judge for forty years until his death, bringing the people back to faithfulness and driving out their enemies.

My father gave us, at our request, part of his inheritance, fields in Hebron. Not long after my marriage, I visited him, to ask for a special gift, trusting that he would remember, and understand. I see him still, strongly upright against a vivid blue sky, for it was before noon and the heat had not turned to whiteness. All around us were the hills, and already the flocks speckled the hillsides, and their cries came drifting down to us. I dismounted from the donkey, handing its reins to my servant, and he strode towards me as I ran to him, so that we met with laughter as well as the courtesy of greeting. *What can I do for you, Acsah, my daughter?* I studied his face and the carving of the years around his eyes and mouth. His gaze was direct and clear, with no sign of ageing or uncertainty. A man who had taken to peace and farming with the same zest that he had brought to the military campaigns of the past years.

Dear Father, I answered. *I ask you for a special favour. You have given me good land to bring to my husband. Now I ask you for the springs that will water that land.* Perhaps he remembered the games of long ago when we would chase through the dry rocks of the wilderness and find, sometimes, the miracle of water breaking from the rock. One such time I remember, where the water welled through a crack in the rocks and he told me that the land that we were going to dwell in drank rain from heaven. That night he told me the story of the great beginning of the earth: the waters above the sky and the waters under the sky from which the dry land came forth. I have thought of that ever since. Perhaps he also remembered, for he said, *I give you the upper and the lower springs.*

That was the last time I saw him alive. Within days, the news reached us that he had died suddenly, in his full strength, shouldering the great stones with which he was to build a wall around the farm. He fell, they told me, with his face turned upward to the light, and it seemed to me when I came to him that I heard the echo of a great laughter in the hills around him. I grieved and all the Tribe with me for many days, and the private loss was something I bore in pain for many months, until the realisation that I carried the first of our babies. This sense of life within brought me strong comfort. Even now, I remember him and the inextinguishable confidence of his hope: *I saw, I know. And it will be.*

His gift to me, my inheritance, was the springs that water the land of our homestead. No woman of our farm ever has to carry far the heavy pitchers of water to supply the household: the lower springs meet our needs even in drought. From the upper springs, the waters well up into pools to water the flocks, and to be run in ditches to supply the needs of the young olive trees and the vines and the barley in the first weeks of its sowing. In the days of my first pregnancy, I used to walk up into the foothills above the springs, looking for that miracle breaking from the rock, the sparkle of light catching the living water. Sometimes Rahab would accompany me, but very soon she married and travelled north and I walked alone, missing her, thinking of the children we would both have and the land that now belonged to them. But soon, the busyness of a growing family overtook my dreaming, and for many years I forgot the paths among the upper springs and the need I had for time apart. A mother and then a grandmother. And I am old now, ageing like my father, outliving my generation, even my husband, and it becomes urgent in me to seek the old paths again and think and dream as I once did, and ponder the meaning of this inheritance. To understand the great mystery of our life, walking as we do between the waters above the earth and the waters beneath it, between the upper and the lower springs of God.

I think of Rahab, dead now for many years, but before her death teaching her children's children the songs of her deliverance and the great truths of her life, never to despise the alien and the foreigner. I think of our mother of faith, Sarah, buried in these hills of Hebron, she who is the mother of us all who dream and hope that our children will dwell in peace. And I think of myself, and of the children I bore and their children, and how women have in their hearts a different inheritance. It is not one carved out of the land by conquest. Our work is to bring life into the world, to see the land flourish, to share our stories and teach our children faith and trust in a God of great and bewildering mystery and yet, I now see, of great closeness. I feel a presence in these hills as I walk, and I think of women like myself, Rahab and Sarah, who yearned that the sons they bore might bring peace as the true inheritance. I dream of a time when the sounds of weeping and slaughter will be silenced for ever. And it is only here, in this place, where I can understand a little of what it means to live between the upper springs of heaven and the lower springs of earth, tasting the water of both.

And so this evening I will take my great grand-daughter on my lap and sing to her, so that she may sing to her children:

Acsah rode on her donkey
To ask for a special gift.
Caleb, my father,
Give to me springs
That will water the field.
The field you have given to me.

And he answered her,
Acsah my daughter
Now and forever,
I give you a gift for your field:
The upper and lower springs
Flowing forever
Between heaven and earth
Will be yours.
Now and forever be yours.

Shaken by the Wind

When I can stretch them out, the tips of my fingers touch the walls on each side. Rough, damp stone, achingly cold in the darkness. Pressing near, as though they might tilt and crush me. The clear air outside, the searching wind from the mountains, the huge swinging patterns of the stars, the blaze of sun, all, all, no longer exist. Water is green and stagnant in the metal dish; food tasteless, clinging dry to the palate and my own spittle barely enough to chew and swallow it. And I shift my position: to stand cramped, to sit hunched, to catch the shaft of grey light that comes in the hours of dawn through the small window high on the wall.

I do not think of her, the woman who sent me here and holds the thread of me between her fingers. She cannot taunt or touch me. Nor do I fear that sly man, her lover, who visits me secretly at night to hear words that he dare not take into the light with him when he leaves my cell. I stare at these walls, waiting for an ending that I know will come. That I do not fear.

And unfamiliar with the keys and locks of memory, I fumble in my heart to let myself re-admit the past.

Our mothers were very close, that I remember. The warmth of them, a gaiety of spirit as they visited one another, sitting together, talking quietly, laughing sometimes, their hands busy with preparation for the meal or the making and mending of clothes. Singing songs that dated back to the shared year of our birth. Reciting, teaching us. Each holding what I see now was a great shared secret of gladness and delight. And a deep contentment in each other's company. Yet my mother died before I reached twelve, and my father a few years later. From the day of her death he became weary with age and was longing, I think, to follow her. But he continued with all his duties and watched over me faithfully until I was old enough to survive alone. I was sixteen, an earnest student, carefully taught and memorising all the traditions, but also free, running wild, they said, over the goat paths of the hill country until I felt that I knew the rocks and scrub of the landscape, the secret springs and streams, better than I knew the yard of my own home. I herded goats, harvested olives and vines for neighbours, learned how to lean into the plough to break up the stony ground and lay it bare for the seed. But all the time, knowing that one day I would leave all this. That I would walk away into the edge of things, and live there, eating and drinking the wind and the wildness, and waiting.

I knew who I was waiting for. As children we had played together, laughing as we chased around the trees, screaming in excitement as we splashed through the streams, scooping up handfuls of brilliant water to splatter one another. Then wrestling until we collapsed breathless in the dust and carried our bruises and scratches home to be fussed over, comforted and then forgotten in the warmth of food and shelter.

A happy childhood. Yet great differences came between us. I was serious beyond my years, an isolate, craving the rigours of the desert landscape, matching my body against the starkness of the scything cold under the bright stars, the heaviness of the sun's heat at the height of the day. The words of Law and prophecy devoured me. I craved the disciplines, withdrawing more and more from relationship, from indulgence, from temptation, until without realising it I had left my family's home empty and lived in the wild places, the desert east of the Jordan. I had been in awe of him, younger though he was, in awe of his profound peace. The sense of depth, the secret energy of his faith, his quiet steady assurance of mission. But his path through childhood and into youth was one of friendship, laughter, even playfulness. What I struggled for—the earnestness of a walk with God, the prophetic calling, the passion and anger that would denounce the wickedness of the age and turn a nation back to righteousness—he took with ease, as you would take ripe fruit from a tree. 'Yes,' he would say, smiling. 'But there is more. The Kingdom is more than judgement. It is grace.' I did not understand, then or now. I knew that he was God-marked, so close to God in his walking that one day he would stride into the very heart of the nation and begin a ministry like no other to call the people back to God.

Under the wilderness skies passionate words filled my mouth as my call came to me: to baptise, to challenge, to call for repentance, to defy the religious rulers who had compromised with the politics of Herod Antipas and Rome. To call for crooked paths to be made straight, for mountains of arrogance to be brought low. The crowds came. Curiosity for the spectacle brought many. Some came desperate for renewal, eager to be baptised, to walk a new path, to seek the restoration of the Kingdom. The months went by: all was in preparation for his coming.

Then, I saw him and knew him as he walked towards me, though we had not talked for many months. I knew this time, this moment, was his: the restoring of the Kingdom. His steps retraced the nation's history as he came down the valley to the Jordan. And I identified him as the one promised, the one about whom the prophets had spoken, the one who would winnow the chaff from the wheat, lay the axe to the root of the tree. Bring the promised judgement and the restoration of Israel. Baptise with the terrible energy of fire. And I was unworthy to untie his sandals.

But what I saw, what he said, demolished me. I saw a terrible simplicity, a vulnerability. A lamb, high-stepping over the rocks towards me with that same playful energy of old, yet carrying already the knowledge of sorrow and sin. 'Look', I said, not knowing what it might mean. 'The Lamb of God, who takes away the sin of the world.' Not the sin of Israel. That is what I would rather have said. Nor the scapegoat of the Day of Atonement. Something new, something alive and charged with energy. Then he came to me, to be baptised. 'To fulfil all righteousness', he said, seriously, but his eyes were laughing. And I remembered the playful games of our childhood, and ducked him beneath the water, splashing him with its brightness in the dazzle of the sunshine. But as he turned from me, waist deep in the pool, I saw the waters running towards him, from way north beyond the Syrian border, water from all the tributaries of the Jordan, deep calling to deep, running over the stones of the river bed, and bloodied from the past slaughter of tribe and tribe, army against army. Bloodied too I saw, with dreadful vision, with the ceaseless warfare of the generations that would follow us, flowing down from the northern heights to run south to the Dead Sea. And he waded through its flow. Then, as he stepped into the shallows and onto the bank, I saw the water running fresh again, the stain vanished as though it had never been.

Then a dove came to him, and I heard the voice, and the love, and the Fathering. Saw the dove, resting on him.

I did not see him after that. He increased, I decreased, and that is right. And yet I feel, as I remember those days, a deep strangeness between us now. I hear of his words. You visit me with news that he preaches, teaches, heals. Yet no triumphant mission that overthrows the rulers, drives out the corruption of the age. Recalls the people to a jealous God. So I said, ask him, for I have lost my certainty. Ask him, are you the One?

Your answer shakes me. The blind see. The lame walk. Lepers are whole again. The poor hear good news. The signs of the Messiah. Blessed are those who do not fall away because of me. And so I must begin again. To seek to understand, to see clearly in a place where there is no light, where there is no wind to stir the spirit.

So I set myself, in the grey half-light of each day, and in the blank darkness as night falls, to remember, to trace the river back to its spring. To recall the songs and stories taught us as children. Their chant, half-murmuring song, half-whispered story, comes to me again out of the long past into this emptiness of the heart. My own father's song as my mother sung it with her cousin, long ago. He has visited and redeemed his people. A visitor, a guest. And we a nation trampled under the heavy feet of conquerors, invaders. How can such a one claim his kingdom, restore his people?

The air changes.

A door has opened at the head of the stairs and the breeze touches me, a coolness that for a moment carries the scent of herb and animal, the outside world. The stench of my own clothes and body, the stale and stinking air of the prison, of all of us stifled here, is ruffled and scattered just for a moment by the sweetness of that breath. Then I hear the silence, the way birds fall quiet before the storm, the earth holds its breath before rain. The secret of the jail, the instinctive hush of prisoners before even the first footsteps of the guard slam down the stone stairs, rhythmic, remorseless. Grinding the heavy keys and latch of my door, fastening the chains at wrist and ankles, taking me at last into the upper air.

Freshness of the light wind. Huge night sky visible above the courtyard wall.

Beyond the animal fear, that trembles in my legs and dries my mouth, I feel a great and sudden gladness.

Returning

Hannah brought warm water for my feet. The lavender she had steeped in it soothed them and the scent filled my head with remembered gentleness. It was easy to cry. She cried too and we shared the towels, my feet, her eyes and mine, crying and laughing together. An old nurse can break down all your defences with one word or touch. Then they brought sandals, new leather, soft on graze and bruise.

I was surrounded with laughter and welcomes. The older servants strong and genuine in their greetings, the ones new to the household less certain and holding back, and some I saw drift to my brother as if seeking his approval. But over all, there was my father, his voice strong and clear above the hubbub, clapping his hands and sending the servants scurrying and calling for the cook to hurry the feast. I saw him then as if every detail was fresh and new to me. Older, yet filled with zest and humour, striding around the courtyard. His hands strong and wide, gesturing with energy, arms that could grip powerfully, his broad wrestler's body planted on strong feet. Mostly I saw his face. The years of my absence had taken a toll; grey dominated black in the hair of beard and temples. His mouth, wide now with laughter and instructions, showed little change, but tracks of pain showed on his forehead and around his eyes. The face of a man who had scoured the horizon against the sun's intensity, I thought, and I saw him again, standing on the road outside the village, searching the far distance for me.

For a moment, the ring felt cold and strange on my signet finger and then warmed to the warmth of my hand. The cloak swept round me, covering the filthy and shameful tunic of my travels, and I was again crushed against my father's chest, his hands clapping my shoulders exuberantly, but he was speechless now. I felt the sob of his diaphragm against my own.

The meal came: meat, flat bread and herbs, honey cakes and fruit, piled up on platters for everyone—household and servants, anyone who had heard the news. I had somehow washed and wore clean clothes and made some effort to greet my father's guests but my legs began to shake with weariness. My father's arm steered me to a bench and he sat with me, answering the questions, laughing. I must have fallen asleep against him and woke to hear guests call out their thanks under a sky hung with stars. I remembered with a twist of pain and shame that once they had seemed so crisp and clear that I could reach out for them, seize them like jewels and spend them recklessly. Now I saw their unwavering remote patterns against an obsidian sky.

My brother had gone to check the night watch for the flock. We had not spoken since my arrival. I had heard the tone but not the words of his reaction. Always there had been envy, a simmering resentment of my birth that broke into fighting as soon as I found my legs. My mother died soon after I was born and perhaps that too turned him against me. I had felt the need to measure up to his competence, his assured rightness about everything. I learned to shrug and then find ways to subtly undermine his achievement. By the time I had dishonoured my father and demanded my share of the inheritance, we loathed each other.

How can I describe the days that followed my return? My father's joy was warmth and light to the whole household. My brother stayed out, striding the hills some said, struggling to adjust to this brother whom he thought and wished was dead, but who had come back from the grave. I saw my father seek him out and sit beside him, gently, gently pleading and responding.

I mended slowly, the body first. Clothes, easy against the skin, food and drink for hunger and thirst, water to cleanse the body. My mind took longer. Amidst the shame there was also great sorrow. Friends had turned away from me as the money and wine and laughter dwindled away. The labour and slow starvation of the last six months had broken something within me. But there were also people that I'd betrayed and abandoned. There were girls who came flocking when the money flowed and left as quickly when it ran out. But there were others, when I was less experienced in seduction, who had believed my promises and were kind and generous to me. I had left them behind in my headlong race of pleasure, and perhaps, perhaps, there was a debt to pay, maybe even a child to acknowledge.

When at length I spoke with my father I watched his response.

'I could send a trusted servant to make enquiries.'

'No,' I had answered. 'It has to be me. There are debts to pay, and ruined lives that I must find and mend. No-one should be outside the kind of homecoming you offered me. I will return to you, father. But first I must go back to where I left a trail of harm and see what can be healed.'

'There is room in my house for all the broken fragments of your life,' he said, gazing into my eyes very steadily. 'Go, my son.'

I left in the grey dawn of the next day, under an arch of fading stars. The sun's barely visible light touched the olive boughs with silver and awoke the birds, and I heard their song and chatter and the calls of sheep and goats from the far hillside as I walked down the road, retracing the steps of the man I once was.

The Leftovers

I

She was born early, my precious daughter, early and frail. More than ten years after our thriving sons. Long-desired by me after many miscarriages, but conceived in indifference by my husband. He had found other satisfaction than a tired wife, but he loved his sons and had proudly taken them to his shipyard and set them to watch and learn his trade and skills. My daughter struggled for life, left to me and my maid to guard day and night to see her feed and grow. But as her eyes opened and she saw the world, it was as if it filled her with terror. As if she had no skin to cover her from the heat of the sun or the weight of the darkness. Her screams would fill the courtyard, and as she learned to crawl and walk she would rush in panic, scrabbling into corners, hiding even from those who loved her most. My husband shrugged. *Silence her,* he said. *Get doctors or priests. She brings shame on our house.* Her only quietness came when she slept, and that mostly curled up in my lap, or that of my dear maid.

Between us we kept her safe and helped her grow for seven years, letting only our gentle family physician near her, and hiding her even from her brothers whose clumsy kindness caused her to grip her head and begin to beat it against the door. I knew what sort of remedies the priests would bring; incantations and bloodletting. But I also knew, one day, she would awaken out of her nightmares and live. Sometimes I glimpsed in the dark wells of her eyes that there was a plea for help, a promise of love. Each day we spent hoping, refusing to give way to despair.

Behind the veils that we must wear, we women watch and listen. We store up memories and stories of truth and kindness together, sharing the distresses, the pains of childbirth or barrenness, the unloving intimacies of marriage. News flows between us because of our trust, and there is an eagerness to help each other in crisis and comfort one another in need that keeps us alive. You know nothing of it, if you are free to walk and talk wherever you choose. But between us, there is a current of life. That current flowed freshly to me in the early spring of my daughter's seventh year, bringing news from the south, across the blood-soaked border between our two nations. A man like no other, it was rumoured, who spoke kindly to women, welcomed children, sought no-one's approval and no power for himself. A man who seemed more fully alive, more free in what he said and did than others. Who talked of God but not religion, loved his friends but excluded no-one, not even beggars, or prostitutes, from the experience of his kindness. There were miracles of healing, demons driven out, and lepers touched and restored. Some spoke snatches of his words, heard and overheard in the market-place and at the well, and none of them seemed to fit into the tight recitations of our priests. So I dared to hope. If he should come north, beyond Galilee, across the northern border into Syria, I would take a servant and leave my daughter in the safe keeping of my maid, and travel from the edge of Tyre to find him. And I would beg him to show kindness to us, for the sake of his ancestor King David, who had once been a friend of King

Hiram of Tyre. For the sake of that ancient alliance, I would beg him for the life of my little girl.

So I pleaded in the dust, a foreign woman, begging him, *Son of David, heal my daughter, tortured as she is by an unknown torment, heal her, you who are more than man, heal her, Lord!* How I reached his feet I do not know. My servant, holding the donkey and sworn to secrecy, stood far away by the well, afraid of this close group of men who had a palpable sense of comradeship, and were tough and swarthy from sun and wind.

It was a time beyond time: I do not know how long. A silence as they looked at me, all of them, and then a murmur of hostility. *Send her away! How dare you come near us, whining for pity! Get away, woman. Canaanite bitch!* Jagged words like stones. Only the thought of my child, and the stillness and silence of the man whose feet I touched, helped me to bear their disgust and contempt. I felt it beat in my ears even when they fell silent.

Then he spoke. Not to me. Not to them. To himself? I do not know. Nor do I understand the emotion that was buried in his words. *I was sent to the lost sheep of Israel.* And around him there was a satisfied murmur of assent.

Then a wonderful thing. He looked fully at me, and I saw him take the stone words they had thrown at me as I had once seen a magician in childhood take a pebble and toss it in the air, and it became a bird that flew away singing. *You know,* he said, and the corners of his mouth quirked with laughter and his eyes dared me to rise to his challenge, *it surely can't be right to take the food from the children and throw it to their pet dogs!*

I felt life stir in me, as sure and strong as a baby kicking in the womb. *Yes, Lord, you're right,* I answered, with a boldness no woman should show to a man, let alone a foreign stranger. *But in the family, the children feed their pet dogs with the crumbs that are left over from the table.*

And you are right! He answered, laughing aloud, and shouting with approval. *What an answer! What faith!* He looked round at his companions. *Do you hear what this woman says? It breaks down old barriers!* And he turned back to look at me, and bent down to raise me up with one hand. *You will have more than left-over crumbs. Go home. Your daughter is well.* I knew it was true. And I remember, as though that yesterday is always today, the way he laughed and spun round on his heel and headed for the southern road, seizing two of his friends by the shoulders and calling the rest to come with him.

I ran to my servant and swung onto the donkey's back, jabbing with my heels to urge him forward on the road home. I found my daughter peacefully sleeping with her head in the lap of my maid, and as I came to her she stirred and put out a hand to me, and her eyes, as they opened, were full of light.

II

I watched him turn away, laughing, his head thrown back and neck arched as though sharing the joke with the sky and the distant mountains. He flung an arm around Simon Peter's stiff shoulders. *You don't understand what is happening, do you? But you will, you will!* And he thrust Peter forward, seized Andrew on the left and began the sidestepping dance of men at the grape harvest. His mood was irresistible and they swung together, caught up in his laughter as we turned away from the road to Tyre and began the journey south. To the south west, over the Great Sea, heavy clouds were gathering like linen sheets swelling and billowing with the weight of the spring rains.

I do not know which of us spat those insults at her. I tend to seek the edge of the crowd, even of this group of close friends, and to watch and wait rather than plunge into the mood of the moment, and I have been called *dog* myself often enough to feel an uneasy kinship with the woman as the words were flung. Sitting at the counting desk, receiving the taxes, loathed by my countrymen, despised by the occupying army, I had been spat at. I felt with her but never dreamed that she could answer as she did, nor that her answer would be so approved. Her healing, I realise, began mine also, dogs together, but raised up by laughter. So I understood a little as we hurried south, just a little, of the overturning of the old order, the rediscovery of the bonds of man and man, man and woman, that could overcome boundaries and histories of cruelty and suspicion.

All my life I have been a man who loved to deal in substance, what can be held in the hand, listed in a column of figures, seen and grasped, felt in the flesh. The weight and slide of coinage, the scrape of stylus, the ease that comes with water as the feet are washed after a hot and dusty day. After I was called away from the counting desk, I took pleasure in a new and amazing comradeship with a host of different sensations, the arm flung around the shoulder, the shared wineskin, the rough bread breaking open, the sparks crackling from the thorn bush fires after dark. Most delight came when I saw and felt beneath my fingers the tormented flesh heal, the puckered scars smooth, the emaciated limbs gain flesh and muscle. I held in my hands bread of texture and flavour that broke and broke again and fish that softened and split to be handed out to feed a multitude. It was within my hands: I picked up the fragments that were left over, and counted the baskets full of food still fragrant, crisp, edible. Twelve baskets. Unforgettable moments of elation where we saw a King feed his people, a kingdom restored to the twelve tribes again.

But then, bewilderment. No sweeping movement of triumph, but the steady retreat into privacy, away from the clamour of the crowd, north across the border to Syria. Just one encounter there and one miracle, and words that puzzled, even disturbed us, as we set out along the road that would take us back to Galilee. What followed then, I began to understand and see as a pattern. Only now, remembering, sharing, does it fully come together, and I recognise that the encounter with the woman was a pivot, a turning point from old and familiar into the unknown, the incalculable.

The crowds gathered with their endless pitifulness of sickness and maiming of soul and body, their hunger and weariness, and again the challenge: *how will you feed them?* We had learned not to say *send them away.* The memory of our experience in Syria had made those words uncomfortable in our mouths, and so we waited. And again, the miraculous food: the bread (and even now I can feel in my hands the way it broke, crust cracking and dough pulling apart) and the small fish, given away again and again to the desperate hands. And I remember the eyes of the crowd, men, women, children, eyes dark and unnaturally large with hunger and with longing. And in the evening we had gathered up seven baskets of what was left.

I know the meaning and texture of numbers. Twelve for the twelve tribes: even, balanced, complete, like a rounded column of figures, a pair of scales exactly balanced. Twelve to restore the ancient kingdom, to bring back the past and the old certainties. But seven? Uneven, indivisible, the number of perfection, the number of mystery. This lay beyond calculation: it stood for completeness, the perfect and all-sufficient total. Here, in my hands again, the symbol of bread that gave me understanding.

I can see the woman in my mind and hear her answer and his laughter, and with it my own voice, *I see! I see!* And feel the shaking laughter that began that day and will never end.

Seven baskets of leftovers: enough for all the children and all little dogs in the world.

The Tree

'How did he know my name?'

The old man lingered, smiling as an inner world opened behind his eyes, more vivid than the present. I have learned to wait for the stories to come slowly, tasted afresh as they are told. Many people begin with what for them is a mystery and their story is a slow unravelling of a thread. My patients too, begin with what is for them the moment of change, the tipping place where their symptoms began to gather into something which cannot be borne. So I have learned to wait and watch the movement of hands and shoulders and read the script of lines around the mouth and eyes.

This man sat on a bench by the wall, under the shade of a great tree. Beyond him I could see the rough grey-pink hills with their clumps of rock rose, oregano and lavender, and in the far distance a group of sighing pines. A lizard scuttled into a crack in the rock. His head moved at the faint flicker of sound and his hands touched the stick that leaned beside him. As his head turned I saw the milkiness of his eyes and recognised the cataracts of old age. 'You will find him,' they had said, 'by the wall under the tree. We share food and water at midday, and bring him back with us at dusk. Clement sits with him for much of the morning.' And I had found him, comfortable in the afternoon sunlight, a short, round man, with tufted white hair, a face crinkled with lines that could have been concentration and irritation, but which were instantly redeemed by the play of laughter and kindness in his words and expression. He sat there, listening to the quiet wind, the bird calls, the bleating and bells of far-off goats.

'I have come to hear your story', I said, bringing out of my bag what I needed to make notes, and sitting alongside. 'They told you I was coming?'

He nodded and smiled. 'You are collecting the stories for a book, they told me. It is long ago, and in a different land. But I can remember.' And then he said it, the key to his memory. 'How did he know my name?'

I waited for him.

'Names.' He shrugged his shoulders. 'They matter, you know, more than parents realise sometimes. My name, even when I was a child, was shortened. Spoken lovingly, a shortened name is affectionate, but in the mouth of contempt it is spat out. That is how it became. I was very short, you see, even when a child, I was small and a little clumsy, and other children did not want to play with a boy who slowed them down. So I learned to hide, and to dodge behind walls and to climb trees out of sight. I could pretend then that I did not need play or company. When I grew older I learned other ways of hiding. Money.' He laughed and spread his hands. 'If you make enough you can hide behind it. I soon realised that it gave me power and other people needed me—to show them generosity, or make them a loan, or let them off a debt. A pleasant feeling, even when you work for the occupying power and collect their taxes. I realised that there was a kind of pleasure even in hearing my name spoken with fear. Over twenty years I gathered money, built up hatred, saw a slow retribution being worked out for every moment of bullying, even for my father's rejection of me. I knew what I was doing, but there was no way out of the web I had woven for myself. Like a spider. No-one comes calling for fear of being devoured.'

A woman from the house brought us water and wine, bread and olives. We broke the bread together and for a while he sat still in the painful memory of that loneliness. He stirred, his eyes turning as if to search my face for understanding, acceptance. 'I know,' I said. 'Doctors have power like that, to bring healing or to predict death.'

'You understand then. The fascination of power and its loneliness. I married and we had three children, two daughters and a son. My wife died soon after my daughters were married. Of loneliness, perhaps, or the shadow of the hatred that neighbours felt for me and for my work. Dear soul, she never knew. I never told her of my growing discontent. My son left home after her death. He asked for money to travel. I have never seen him since, and that is nearly thirty years ago. There was a story, you know, about the son who ran away and returned to his father. But that was not our story.' He was very still. I poured wine into cups for us both and we drank together.

'I began to leave the town and go to Jerusalem. Searching perhaps, but hiding from those who knew me. Looking for what? I couldn't have given it a name. Something had stirred in me from childhood, the memorised Scriptures, though they brought no comfort. I remembered Amos—he said, "You have sold the righteous for silver and the needy for a pair of shoes". I hung around the outer courts of the Temple, hopelessly crying out, "God have mercy on me", realising that I had nothing left of any worth at all. Week after week I would make that journey, rough and dangerous though it was, just to be in a place where I thought maybe God might hear me. One day I heard a different voice, not a priest or scribe, a man who told a story about a Pharisee and a tax collector, and the tax collector spoke my words, "God have mercy on me". How did he know that? He gave me hope. He said that the man went home accepted by God. He told other stories too, this Teacher, about the Jericho road and the priest and Levite that left the wounded man to his fate. I will tell you that story before you go.'

I watched carefully and recognised the tell-tale breathlessness and greyness around the mouth and nostrils. 'Do not rush this,' I said to him gently. 'I can stay as long as you need. I am just glad to find you and have this chance to hear you.' He put down his cup, and sat more easily, his hands resting for a while, but soon eloquent with gesture as he began to speak.

'It was some weeks after that. The whole town knew that this Teacher was approaching down the road from the old town to the new. There was a great outcry as old blind Bartimaeus begged for his healing and the crowd stopped and saw him healed. I was on the edge, watching, hoping. Not knowing how I could ever get close to this man who had spoken my words, who didn't seem to bring the heaviness of the Law with him to condemn me. I've never seen such a crowd, pressing down the road towards the narrow streets of the town. I tried to push through to see, but there was no space, and then I was recognised by one of the men who owed me money, and he cursed and shoved me away. I moved away from the crowd to the tree—a great sycamore-fig tree by the side of the road which I used to climb as a boy—and climbed it to give me a view over the heads of the crowd. I felt like a child again. You could hear and feel the roar of excitement as the Teacher and his companions approached the town.

They came into view, and stopped, stopped right under the tree and he called to me. "Zacchaeus, come down. I've come especially to visit your house." Everything, everyone, was silent as I climbed down. There were mutters of resentment from the crowd as I led him to my house, but they died away. I spoke very carefully, knowing this was the end of my old life. "I'm giving back everything that I've taken wrongly—four times over. I'm giving half my money and goods to the poor." Can you imagine what he said to me? "Salvation and healing have come to your house today. And do you know who you truly are? You are a true son of Abraham. I have come to find and help desperate people like yourself."

His smile flooded his features, washing away the lines of age and distress. Once again, I waited for him to resume his story in his own time. 'I dealt with the business as soon as possible. I had not realised what it would be like to see a family restored, a widow fed, a beggar lifted back into work and dignity again. I heard the cry of the needy. I had not realised in all my search for money that giving it away was better than keeping it.' He shrugged expressively. 'Soon I went to Jerusalem, and I was there in those amazing days of resurrection and Pentecost, and I helped—they would not have believed it in Jericho!—with the distribution to the poor in those early days of sharing everything. Then I wanted to travel. I think at heart I wanted to search for my son. I brought gifts to the churches and carried letters, visited almost all those small communities of believers. Then I came here, and found a new home. I have not found my son, but I have become part of a family. I helped Lydia with her accounts until my eyes failed, and live here in Clement's house. Do you know Clement's story? He wasn't called Clement when he was the town jailer!' We laughed together. 'Names, you see. They mean everything.'

The sun had begun to slip towards the mountains and as the shadows lengthened a chill breeze began to stir the dust across the courtyard. Overhead the leaves stirred. 'You will tell these Jericho stories? Perhaps my son will read them, or his children, and know the truth.' Then he reached out a hand to me and sought my face with his blind eyes. 'Tell me, Doctor Luke,' he asked, 'It won't be long?'

'No,' I answered, understanding his meaning. I took his hand in my left, and with my right hand reached to feel the stammering pulse in his neck. I listened to his shallow breath. 'No, dear friend, it won't be long.'

'That is good,' he said. 'I will be waiting, here, under this tree, for him to come.' Even in the growing dusk, his face was lit again with memory. 'He will call me by name again, I think. But this time it will be his house that we go to.'

Lightning Source UK Ltd.
Milton Keynes UK
UKOW05f0235080114

224126UK00001B/222/P